Dear Reader,

I am a strong believer in family. In the bonds it creates and the needs it meets. But family can look so many different ways, and I wanted to show brothers whose relationship is as strong as any other, even with no DNA between them. Knox and Jackson are tied together forever, and giving them their happily-ever-afters was a dream come true.

Dr. Knox Peters is a winner. In fact, he's come in second only once. And when the woman he lost to shows up in his hospital, Knox is more than a little miffed that Miranda gave up *his* dream. But when sparks fly and challenges resume, can he finally recognize what should have been easy to see all along? He's more than the words on his résumé.

Dr. Miranda Paulson burned bright then burned out. Working hard was her superpower...until suddenly it wasn't. Returning home felt like the right move, but working with Knox brings out less rivalry and more butterflies these days. Can they finally put the competition behind them to find their happily-ever-after?

Juliette Hyland

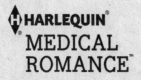

HARLEQUIN®
MEDICAL ROMANCE™

Recycling programs
for this product may
not exist in your area.

ISBN-13: 978-1-335-59540-9

Dating His Irresistible Rival

Harlequin Enterprises ULC
22 Adelaide St. West, 41st Floor
Toronto, Ontario M5H 4E3, Canada
www.Harlequin.com

Printed in U.S.A.

Dating His
Irresistible Rival

JULIETTE HYLAND

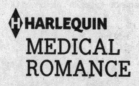

◆ HARLEQUIN
MEDICAL
ROMANCE

Juliette Hyland began crafting heroes and heroines in high school. She lives in Ohio with her Prince Charming, who has patiently listened to many rants regarding characters failing to follow the outline. When not working on fun and flirty happily-ever-afters, Juliette can be found spending time with her beautiful daughters, giant dogs or sewing uneven stitches with her sewing machine.

Books by Juliette Hyland

Harlequin Medical Romance

Boston Christmas Miracles

A Puppy on the 34th Ward

Neonatal Nurses

A Nurse to Claim His Heart

The Vet's Unexpected Houseguest
The Prince's One-Night Baby
Rules of Their Fake Florida Fling
Redeeming Her Hot-Shot Vet
Tempted by Her Royal Best Friend

Harlequin Romance

Royals in the Headlines

How to Win a Prince

Visit the Author Profile page
at Harlequin.com for more titles.

For found families everywhere.

CHAPTER ONE

DR. KNOX PETERS grabbed the soda from the bar and pointed to the back wall. "Game of darts? Loser buys the next round?"

Jackson Peters, his best friend, roommate and for all the purposes Knox cared about, brother, rolled his eyes. "You haven't lost a game since before we met in the boys' home. That hustle might work on the unsuspecting but come on, Knox."

They'd been thrown together in foster care. Bunkmates because of a shared last name. A twist of fate that led to a lifelong friendship.

"Fine. Winner buys the drinks." His buddy was down. Had been down since he returned from Hawaii almost a year ago now. The longest melancholy streak ever. After a vacation. And he wouldn't tell Knox why.

"If you want to play darts, you can just ask me to play darts." Jackson held up the beer he'd been nursing for the past hour in a mock toast.

Knox rolled his eyes before heading to the dartboard. Jackson was right; it wasn't much of a competition. Knox had started playing darts as part of a hustle for one of his less than stellar foster parents. His eye for detail and need for perfection driving him to master the skill, even though his foster father was using it to fleece money from unsuspecting bar patrons.

The fact that the underage Knox was allowed in the bar and on a first-name basis with the bartender should have been a major red flag. But it never seemed to register with the people his foster father targeted.

Knox passed Jackson the set of red darts. Jackson stepped to the line and tossed the first dart, landing close to the bull's-eye. But not close enough.

That was something Knox loved about Jackson. The man had never beaten him at a game. But he never gave up trying. Never threw a game intentionally to make it go quicker.

The game progressed as it normally did. A few people stepped up to watch them toss the darts.

"Such precision!" A young white woman clapped as she moved toward Jackson. His brother wasn't going to win, but the black man was beyond attractive. Still, Knox knew the beauty's attempt was doomed to failure.

Jackson had never been a playboy, but the man had enjoyed regular dates. Something else that had stopped after the vacation.

"She was cute." Knox grabbed his dart from the bull's-eye.

"You should ask her out." Jackson tilted the beer bottle in his direction again.

Knox shook his head. He'd dated three women

since becoming a surgeon. All three had broken up with him when he made it clear that his patients were his first priority. That wasn't fair to them. He understood that.

In a relationship, your partner deserved to know that they were first in your life. Maybe something was broken in him that he seemed incapable of giving that. The universe battered him in his early days. Abandoned by his mother at eight, in and out of foster care until he'd aged out. Hell, he'd graduated high school top of his class to prove to his last foster family that he wasn't a loser.

Not that they'd ever known. They'd dropped him at the boys' home after he failed eighth grade English. Never mind that he'd spent the year hopeful his mother would finally regain custody only to learn she'd actually given up all parental rights. Not an excuse for failure, however.

They'd promptly forgotten him. Knox would never forget, though. He'd been the best at nearly everything he'd done since.

"She didn't hit on me. She hit on you. Getting out a bit more wouldn't be the worst thing to happen." Knox tossed another dart. Bull's-eye.

"I'm not the only one who could do to spend more time out of the hospital." Jackson threw his dart, striking into the heart of the board where only Knox's darts found purchase—usually. "Bull's-eye."

"Lucky throw." Knox chuckled. Even with the

bull's-eye there was no way for his brother to make up the deficit. "The last time one of us took a vacation, he came back grumpier than ever. Maybe it's not the hospital."

Knox was a general surgeon and Jackson a nurse anesthetist. They practically lived at the hospital. Prior to tonight they'd been on shift for nearly a week straight. It was only because of hospital policy demanding they take a night off, that they were here tonight.

"Yet, a vacation still wouldn't hurt you. Your patients would be fine." Jackson tossed his final dart, just off center.

His patients would be fine. Rationally, Knox knew that but so many of the surgeons and staff saw Hope Hospital as a stepping stone. The focus was on next steps, even if it wasn't in the forefront of their minds. Their hospital was small; it saw many patients that were struggling to make ends meet. They deserved stability, too.

But Knox understood. He'd viewed Hope that way, too—once upon a time. And one day he'd leave, but every time a good opportunity opened, he found an excuse not to put in.

"Hey! Take it outside!" The bartender's voice rose above the cacophony of the bar. Knox saw a few heads turn toward the entrance. No doubt cell phones and crowds would follow the action. He needed no part of it.

"Someone's had too much." Jackson grabbed the darts from the board, handing Knox his.

"Someone has always had too much." Knox raised his final dart. It was a sad truth that many of the people he met in the surgical recovery room were there because of a bad decision, overindulgence in alcohol or drugs…or someone else's overindulgences.

His mother had struggled with addiction. Knox understood the disease from a medical perspective. But understanding the dopamine resistance, the tie-in to stress, anxiety, depression and other untreated mental health conditions didn't negate the consequences for those who loved you.

The sound of glass shattering and screams echoed from the front of the building. Jackson was moving beside Knox. Years of medical training kicking into gear before they registered the cries for medical attendants.

"Call 911." Jackson pointed to a young white man holding up his phone. "Now."

The bartender had likely called, too, but it was too crowded for them to make sure. Besides, another call to emergency services wouldn't hurt.

Three bodies lay outside on the sidewalk; blood was already pooling around them.

"Damn." The expletive slipped from his mouth as he took in the scene. The movies made falling through glass look like a quick hit. Maybe a scratched cheek or blood traipsing down the arm before the hero got up and beat the villain.

The actual result was nothing like that.

A white woman was bent over one of the patients, dark curly hair falling over her face as she held pressure on a wound that was seeping blood and fluid. "I'm a doctor. Those two went through the window. She has a stab wound."

Her voice sounded familiar, but it might be the adrenaline. Knox took in the appearance of the two men on the ground. One was conscious. He pointed to him, and Jackson bent to assess while Knox focused on the young white man who was unconscious.

He heard sirens in the distance and hoped they'd sent more than one ambulance. "I've got an unconscious man who is probably midtwenties. Head wound, cuts on the back. Looks like he was first through the window. Pulse rapid but steady. What's her situation?"

Triage in the field was not something surgical staff did often, but they needed to prioritize the first transport.

"I've got a twenty-three-year-old female. Two stab wounds, one to the side and another to the lower abdomen. Pulse thready. She goes first." The female physician's voice was strained. Stab wounds were bad, stab wounds to the abdomen very bad. The young woman would need emergency surgery, and even that might not save her.

"Agreed." Knox looked to Jackson. His patient was sitting up, his face pale, sweat pooling on his forehead, a nasty cut on his left forearm and cuts along his legs. The man's gaze never left the female patient. He was the third transport.

"Will she be all right?" The man had tears running down his cheeks that Knox thought were because of the woman on the ground, not his wounds.

The female doctor didn't look up. Pressure needed to be kept on the woman's wounds. The fact that she didn't answer was not a good sign.

"She'll go to Hope Hospital. It's closest. They'll do the best they can." Knox knew the words weren't comforting, but offering false hope wasn't a great idea, either.

"That's her ex-husband. The bastard was mad she was out with me."

"Take a deep breath for me. I don't want you going into shock." Jackson's voice was soft, but Knox knew his brother's tone. One did not work in healthcare without seeing the effects of domestic violence. DV cases always got to him, but he never let anyone except Knox know that.

Jackson looked at Knox before turning his attention back to the man he was treating. "The police will be informed, but right now our priority is taking care of you all."

There was truth in that. If the man Knox was treating had committed a crime, even a deadly one, it was still their responsibility to treat him.

First, do no harm.

The first ambulance pulled up and the female doctor raised her head. Recognition poured through Knox. Miranda Paulson. No. She was on the East Coast. Working at a fancy research hospital with huge donors. His dream job.

The one he'd have left Hope for—if it had been offered.

"She goes first! Let Hope know to have a surgical suite on standby." Miranda's orders were staccatos in the night. She stood, keeping pressure on the wound like a pro as she walked beside the paramedics and climbed in behind them.

Another ambulance pulled up. Good. Hopefully, one for Jackson's patient would arrive shortly. "My guy next." Knox called over the paramedics. He gave the basics to them and relayed that there might be law enforcement at the hospital.

When the third transport arrived, he waited while Jackson repeated the same measures as he did and passed his patient off to the paramedics.

"Hey, anyone know whose purse this is?" A young black man was holding up a large bag. One that no one would carry into a bar. It was professional, boring and it screamed Dr. Miranda Paulson.

If she had ever cracked a smile during residence, Knox hadn't seen it. And the two were together most of the time. Competing for surgical time, positions and then the follow-on at the research hospital.

Jackson had joked once that they spent more time together than many married couples—and fought like them, too.

"It's Dr. Paulson's."

Knox held out his hand and the man started to give him the purse before pulling back.

"Your hands are covered in blood." The young man shook his head as he held the purse against his chest.

"Right." Good call. Miranda had great taste in clothes. The bag was probably some fancy thing. "Let me clean up, then my colleague and I will head to the hospital. Dr. Paulson will be there. Just give me one minute." Knox looked at his jeans, blood covered the knees, and his shirt was likely ruined, too, but at least he could wash his hands.

"Expensive night out." Jackson ran his hands under the faucet next to him. "Did you say Dr. Paulson?"

"I did." Knox swallowed the other words that bubbled up. He'd recognize Miranda until the day he died. The soft dark curls. Chestnut-brown eyes. Lips that looked like the universe designed them to smile but were in a constant frown. A brain that worked faster than any he'd ever seen.

Jackson cleared his throat but didn't say anything.

"I assume she'll be at the hospital and once the

adrenaline wears off, she'll realize she doesn't have her purse. So we'll run it to her." Knox laid out the plan, ignoring the pinch in his belly at the thought of seeing Miranda again. The woman had gotten the thing he wanted most.

Granted, she'd earned it.

He might have grumbled for weeks about losing the opportunity, but he couldn't ignore that she'd been a good choice.

The better choice.

And he'd redoubled his effort to prove himself. To make himself the best general surgeon at Hope Hospital. Completed his surgical critical care certification and several others, too. Outside of the chief surgeon, Knox had more certifications than any other general surgeon at the hospital.

They headed out of the bathroom. The young man with the bag held it out. "You'll make sure it gets to her?"

"We will. We go way back with Dr. Paulson." Knox heard Jackson cough, but he ignored the sound. They did go way back. Maybe not as besties, but there was a history there.

"Can you play nice?" Jackson looked at the bag in Knox's hands then met his brother's gaze.

"Of course. She's probably just passing through town. Maybe visiting family." She'd had a big family. Three sisters and two happy parents. He remembered them standing together after the white coat ceremony.

Posing for pictures. Jackson had stood in the place of his family that day. Jackson's presence was far better than if his mother had decided to show. But as he saw others basking in their families' warm glow it was hard to ignore jealousy's pinch.

"All right. Let's go find Dr. Paulson."

This wasn't the way Dr. Miranda Paulson planned to return to Hope Hospital. Well, she hadn't actually planned to return at all. No, this was a setback.

A necessary one, maybe. But that didn't change the fact that she'd burned bright at Parkins Research Hospital in New York—a private research hospital that claimed to only employ the best. And she'd flamed out in a well of burnout following her divorce.

Well, actually, the burnout started long before the divorce.

Stepping back, coming home. Restarting. This was not the plan for the former valedictorian of every graduating class she'd been in.

"Dr. Paulson." Hugh Lawton, the head of surgery at Hope, looked far more tired than she remembered. She and Knox Peters had served under him as residents.

Knox. He'd been at the bar tonight. Jackson, too.

Where one went the other followed. Some things never changed. That was oddly comforting. The men weren't brothers, but they were closer than she and her sisters. Blood might be thicker than water, but love was thicker than anything.

And its absence… Its absence was felt through generations. Though they were trying to break that generational curse now. Thirty-plus years late was better than never.

"I'd say it's nice to see you again, before I officially start tomorrow but…" She held up her hands. They were free of blood now, but there were stains on her jeans, and her white tank top was already in the trash. Luckily, a nurse had offered her a fresh shirt from the Hope Hospital laundry. It didn't fit well, but it was free of blood. That was all that mattered.

"Yeah. Riding in on an ambulance with a stab-wound patient might be one for the record books."

"One I'd happily never repeat. Any word on Jill?" The woman had drifted in and out of consciousness in the ambulance. But each time she was awake, she'd begged Miranda to save her.

Words that never got easier to hear.

"Surgery will take hours. Two abdominal wounds…" Hugh's voice floated away.

She knew the stats. He knew she knew the stats. Pulling through surgery was just the first hurdle. The good news was Jill was young. If given the chance, her body would heal faster.

Her surgeons just had to beat the fates for that chance.

"Starting tomorrow you will be on the floor full-time. It's nice to have you home."

"Happy to be here." They were the words Miranda was supposed to say. That they didn't ring true didn't matter. She'd said some version of them many times since turning in her notice at Parkins Research Hospital.

Excited for a new chapter.
Here's to new adventures.
Stepping back will be nice.

Platitudes people expected. Words that hid the imposter syndrome and failure that crawled through her mind nearly every waking minute. The reminder that she had been good, but not good enough.

Hugh nodded. "Never thought we'd see you back in our regional hospital. But I'm glad you're here."

"Miranda!" Knox's voice echoed behind her.

She turned and her body did what it always did. Locked down.

The man was mouthwateringly handsome. Smart. Humorous. She always told friends that doctors didn't look like they did on television. Not all six-packs and smoky gray eyes that made you want to strip the scrubs from their bodies.

Dr. Knox Peters would fit in perfectly on the set of any television drama. Except he was a brilliant surgeon.

They'd competed for everything from college through med school and residency. Her first. Him second…barely. The man should have done a year or two at Hope and then moved on to a bigger hospital.

Hell, she'd half expected to find him next to her at Parkins someday. Maybe if he had…

She forced her mind to walk away from the what-if. Knox was here, walking up to her. Jackson beside him. Holding her purse.

Her hand went to her hip. She'd changed her shirt and not realized her purse was still at the bar.

Brains on autopilot could do miraculous things while dumping all information it deemed unnecessary during fight-or-flight mode. Like not having her purse.

"Thank you. How are your patients?" She took the purse from Knox's hands, careful to avoid touching him. Her body had lit up once upon a time when he touched her. Light touches, professional. Nothing sexual, but her body hadn't been able to tell the difference.

She was not risking the discovery that the crush was still alive and well. Or rather, she wasn't looking for confirmation.

Her divorce was finalized a year ago. The separation had occurred a year before that.

"One is under arrest, but expected to make a full recovery. The other is getting patched up outside the OR waiting room."

Knox blew out a breath before running a hand through his blond hair. "Rough night." If this was a TV drama, the moment would have been captured on a long camera. The audience sighing at the sight of the hot doc looking troubled over patients. It was so cliche…except Knox wasn't acting.

"It was good the three of us were there. You staying in Phoenix long?" Knox smiled. His top teeth were still just a hair uneven. Her ex-husband would have put caps on them. They didn't take anything away from Knox, though. In fact, she thought they added to his beauty.

"Oh." Miranda looked at Hugh. Had he not told Knox that she was starting tomorrow? Was it because their rivalry had been more than a little too much as residents? That was years ago.

Time might not heal all wounds, but they were hardly student competitors anymore.

"Dr. Peters. Dr. Paulson is our new general surgeon. I told you Dr. Paulson would be shadowing you when she started."

"I didn't think you meant Miranda. She is supposed to be some hotshot on the East Coast."

Was that an inflection on the word supposed?

Miranda bit the inside of her cheek to keep a neutral look on her face.

Don't read into things.

His dark blue eyes caught hers, lightning seeming to flash through them. "Paulson isn't exactly an uncommon name."

Jackson shifted. If frustration was a vibe, it would be Knox's best friend in this moment.

"You got the fellowship. You worked at Parkins Research Hospital. You—"

"Failed and came home." Miranda nodded. "Yep. They should have given it to you." She hefted her purse onto her shoulder. "Hindsight really is twenty/twenty."

"Knox," Jackson's voice was soft but she saw Knox flinch at the tone. A soft-spoken reminder.

Miranda bit her lip. "If you don't want me to shadow you—"

"It's fine." Knox shook his head. "You really gave up the Parkins job? Really?"

"*Gave up* is a relative term." She'd not been fired, but her performance appraisals made it clear they weren't going to renew her contract. So she'd resigned and taken the vacation she'd put off for forever before coming back here.

He cleared his throat. "Sorry."

"Don't be." Miranda crossed her arms. It wasn't much of a defense, but it gave her a small sense of control. "I failed. A first." Her eyes drifted to the floor.

Why did it have to be Knox witnessing the failure? Her parents were gone. Her sisters were happy she was home. They viewed the setback as a gain. A chance to start over.

Only Miranda knew what her failure meant. And it was easy to see when it radiated back from the colleague she'd strangely missed. "Maybe if you'd been there, I could have focused on beating you."

"No one beats me these days."

A startled laugh escaped her chest. "I meant it as a joke." She looked at Hugh and pulled her phone from her back pocket to order a car through the mobile app she'd downloaded when she landed.

"So much for playing nice." Jackson's words were barely audible, but the fact that Knox must have talked about how he would behave before they'd arrived saddened her.

She'd seen them as rivals. As two skilled colleagues trying to best each other. Not enemies.

Of course, I won everything, though.

Maybe that clouded her memories. Either way it didn't matter. "I'll see you tomorrow." Then she pushed past them without looking back. Her soul was too bruised to continue the verbal sparring.

Tomorrow she'd be Dr. Paulson, don the mental armor she'd used all her life. Tough surgeon. Nononsense physician. Top of her class.

Rather than the broken woman she felt like when she was alone.

CHAPTER TWO

MIRANDA SAT IN her car, mentally prepping herself to walk through the doors of Hope Hospital. Today was the first of a new chapter. That this was a chapter she hadn't wanted was irrelevant.

She needed to do her best.

Best. Her parents' favorite word.

Miranda had grown up answering the question: Did you do your best? She'd heard so many parents say some variation of it. But in the Paulson family, *best* had one meaning. Perfection.

The thing was that until she'd left Arizona, Miranda had always met the metric. Exceeded it. Blew past it. Made it look easy when she was breaking inside.

And it hadn't mattered.

Even perfection wasn't enough to make her parents proud. At least not for Miranda. Her sisters weren't as focused on perfection. Maybe it was eldest-daughter syndrome. She'd read that in one of the self-help books she devoured.

Whatever it was, her life had fallen apart at Parkins Research. She had fallen apart. She couldn't hack it.

She closed her eyes, pinching them tight. That was the past. And she was moving forward. No one needed to know.

Except I told Knox last night...and Hugh was there, too. And Jackson.

Just blurted everything out. Hopefully, the hectic events would drown out the memories.

She held her head high as she walked through the doors of Hope. Dr. Miranda Paulson was not going to fail—not again.

"Good morning, Dr. Paulson." Knox's voice was calm as he stepped beside her, waiting for the elevator to arrive in the garage.

"Morning, Dr. Peters." Miranda kept her tone even, waiting for the inevitable questions from last night. Her ex-husband seized on any sign of weakness. Knox had, too, when they were residents. Though in a different way.

Lance was cruel. Knox just used any advantage he could find to come in first. Even if he'd always only managed second place when Miranda was in the game.

"Hugh wants you shadowing me." His words were crisp as the elevator doors opened.

"That was what he said last night." Miranda raised an eyebrow as she met Knox's gaze. She watched his lips move, just a little. Like he was running his tongue over his teeth. A nervous habit?

Knox shifted on his heels. "Yes." He pushed the button for the surgical floor before leaning against the wall of the elevator.

The picture of handsome. So relaxed, though he made the same motion with his mouth again.

Maybe she wasn't the only one acting like nothing bothered her.

"However, after you walked off, I recommended the standard two weeks shadowing be reduced." He crossed his arms before continuing, "After all, you've worked here before."

And it means we have to spend less time together.

Perhaps he wasn't thinking that, but it stung that he'd immediately requested to shorten the time he spent with her.

"True." What else was she supposed to say?

The elevator doors opened, and she sucked in a deep breath. Time to move. Though that wouldn't stop the next week of spending every work moment with Knox.

She started to turn left, but Knox touched her shoulder. His fingers were gone so fast, but Miranda found herself looking at where they'd been.

"Where are you going?"

Pointing to the left she looked at him. Was he tricking her? "The locker room?"

Knox followed her hand then shook his head. "They remodeled the floor two years ago. Locker room is down here now."

"Ah." A remodel. That was nice. The former facilities had been clean, but the old pink tile a clear reminder that the hospital really only funded projects patients saw. Staff locker rooms, supply hallways, storage rooms, those were always decades out of date.

"Maybe you do need two weeks."

"Maybe I do." Miranda knew Knox hadn't expected her to hear his muttered words, but she'd been gone eight years. Things changed. That was good. Change was good. At least according to all the self-help books on her shelf.

Knox's blue eyes held hers, and she stood there, waiting for him to say something. "Let's get changed, then rounds."

"Fine."

Maybe I do.

Knox laid his head against the locker as he tried to force himself to focus on the plan for today. Show Miranda around. Make sure she understood what she needed then let Hugh know that one day was actually enough.

Sure, most got six, two weeks total, since they did three days on and three days off at Hope, unless you picked up extra shifts. But Miranda had been here before. She knew the routine.

She could pick up anything, effortlessly. It was what had made her top of class. Her brain was a machine. His was fast, but most of that was hard work that he hid from everyone but Jackson. Smoke and mirrors designed to look effortless.

Being around her again brought out feelings he hadn't felt in forever. Miranda had always made him try his hardest. She was his foil. Part of him missed the banter. The drive. The need to beat her.

Last night, though, she'd looked different.

Still beautiful. The woman was the definition of gorgeous. Maybe there were a few extra creases around her eyes, but they added to her glory. She still looked like Miranda but the fire, the spark that made her *her*, seemed diminished.

I failed.

Two little words that made him so uncomfortable. He could not imagine a world where Miranda failed. That place didn't exist.

He pushed off the locker. Whatever thoughts were forcing their way through his brain wouldn't do him any good right now. Get Miranda through the day and make sure she was good enough not to need him. That was his only goal.

"I heard your guy from last night was arrested as soon as he regained consciousness." She was leaning against the wall in the hallway, the blue scrubs that seemed to drape over everyone else hugging her so perfectly.

How did she manage that?

"Not surprised." It was unfortunate but not the first time he had a patient with law enforcement escorts. One bad choice could alter everything.

Not enough people thought that through. Or considered who else might be impacted by their issues. His mother never had...or if she did, it didn't make her change her actions.

"My patient came through her surgery." Miranda looked to her feet before looking back at him.

He heard her unstated *but*. Abdominal wounds were tricky. Something every general surgeon knew. With luck, she was done lying on their operating table.

"And her date?"

Miranda smiled. "You can tell Jackson that I saw him on his way to find a cup of coffee. He had sixty stitches spread out on all his appendages but otherwise he is fine. He's stayed with Jill all night. Not the greatest first date."

"First date!" Knox knew his mouth was hanging open. "Man, I've had more than a few rough starts but that really takes the cake."

"Rough starts?" Miranda let out a small chuckle. "How can *you* have a rough start?" Her cheeks darkened as she met his gaze but she didn't withdraw the question.

"It happens to us all. Though maybe not to you." Miranda's strive for perfection probably touched every aspect of her life, dating life included.

"First dates… I can count on one hand the number I've had."

"Only one hand? I've got at least two handfuls of bad first date stories." Yep, perfection, thy name was Miranda.

"Oh." She grabbed a tablet chart from the nurses'

station and shrugged. "No, I've only gone on four first dates. Always too busy, then I met Lance."

"Lance. I remember him. Neuro, right?"

"Right." Miranda didn't look up the from the chart. She wasn't wearing a ring, but then surgeons typically didn't. Still, there was something in her body language.

The set of her lips. The tightness in her shoulders. He'd seen many divorces in his life. Though he didn't remember his mother and father's, more than one foster family had imploded while he was there. And several residents had married and divorced before they'd managed to land at the same hospital.

It happened. Only psychiatry had a higher divorce rate than surgeons.

"So, back at Hope. Must feel like a step down from Parkins Research?" He was proud of the work Hope Hospital did. It was a regional hospital, not internationally known, but the hospital did good work.

"Do you think it's a step down?" Miranda tilted her head, a loose curl falling over her left eye.

He didn't. This place felt nice—that wasn't quite the right word for the feeling that made him turn down every new opportunity offered.

"We've got two crash victims coming in!" Lisa, the charge nurse on the floor called over the radio. "Teens, drag racing. Both have arrested once en route."

All thoughts disappeared as he and Miranda headed for the surgical suites, listening to the stats come over the radio.

"Jackson here today?" Miranda asked over the hum of the water as they scrubbed up.

"Yeah. He'll be in with us. Hugh and Mitchell have Beth as their nurse anesthetist." They gloved up and moved into the OR. The minutes ticked by.

Jackson nodded as he sat monitoring anesthesia equipment that wasn't needed yet.

"I hate this part." Miranda's voice was soft, barely carrying over the light music in the room.

"Me, too." Jackson nodded as he triple-checked the equipment he would use to keep the patient sedated.

Knox wasn't fond of the wait, either. General surgeons saw more trauma than other specialties. That didn't mean the wait was easy.

Commotion echoed in the hallway and the professionals in the surgical suite seemed to take a deep breath together.

"Sixteen. Had to use Jaws of Life to get him out." The ER team rushed the kid in. Reciting stats that weren't great. "Collapsed lungs, internal bleeding…"

The list went on.

Typically, a general surgeon operated with a resident. But since it was Miranda's first day, she was standing opposite him. It was a weird feeling. They'd never worked like this. They'd each stood in the spot where she was, but it was Hugh or one of the other surgeons standing where Knox was.

Her dark eyes met his as he took the scalpel, and a sense of calm settled within Knox. He looked to Jackson and waited for him to give the thumbs-up that the patient was fully under.

"All right, Dr. Paulson, let's get to work."

The teen, Fritz, was in recovery. Touch and go was the name of the game and would be for the next forty-eight hours. She and Knox had closed three lacerations in his abdominal cavity and removed his spleen. His friend had lost his foot above the ankle.

A terrible day for all involved. But the boys were alive.

"Ready to talk to the parents?" Miranda pulled the cap off her curly hair. Her feet were sore, and her lower back ached. It was weird how surgeons just got used to it.

"Nope. But that is what we have to do." Knox pulled his own surgical cap off.

She understood his statement. There was no easy way to tell parents that they still weren't sure if their child would make it. Still, there was something in Knox's eyes, a look that made her heart clench.

"I can do the notification, if you want?"

Knox's eyebrows pulled together as he shook

his head. "I was the lead surgeon. It's my responsibility."

His shoulders straightened a hair on the word *responsibility.*

"All right." She walked beside him. A weird sense of home settling around her. She'd notified hundreds of loved ones in the course of her career. Told people the best and worst news. Today's notification was somewhere in between. But delivering it with Knox—it felt different.

"If you're son hadn't dared my son, he wouldn't have lost his foot!"

"I don't even know what has happened with my son! And your boy has always been a troublemaker. Fritz is a good kid. Straight-A student."

"Oh, please. That's because you can afford to pay off teachers."

"I do not!"

The argument poured through the doors to the waiting room. Adult voices blending together in a cacophony of blame.

"Blame game already started." Miranda sighed. Both boys were alive. That was no small miracle considering they'd crashed at high speeds. But it was human nature to want to blame someone.

"Never a good sign." Knox rolled his head from side to side, then stepped through.

Two white women were standing, noses nearly touching, both with tearstained cheeks. They turned almost in unison and Miranda knew her eyes were wide as the identical twins stared at her and Knox.

"Fritz?" The woman on the right teetered and her sister wrapped a hand around her waist. The argument forgotten, at least for the moment.

"He came through surgery but the next twenty-four hours will be touch and go." Knox took a deep breath, his body shifting a hair closer to Miranda. "We had to remove his spleen."

"His spleen." The woman who was clearly Fritz's mother slipped to the floor. "Can you live without that?"

"Yes," Knox stated and Miranda looked at him, waiting for him to expand on that a little more.

When he didn't, she took a step forward. "A normal life, though he might be more prone to infection. My sister had hers out due to a car accident a few years ago. She has a scar but otherwise no issues."

"So he will be all right?" Her watery eyes met Miranda's and she realized her misstep.

Kelly's accident wasn't as extensive as Fritz's and her recovery took months. Fritz wasn't stable enough for her to make promises. It was a misstep she'd have never made a year ago. Her ability to distance herself from the trauma, from the reactions, a necessary trait in surgeons, was broken.

"We will be better able to give a prognosis tomorrow afternoon. Right now, he is stable." Knox's words were controlled, commanding, but Fritz's mother refused to let her gaze leave Miranda's.

"Promise me he is going to be okay."

There was no way for Miranda to offer that promise. "We are doing everything we can." Words that she doubted were much comfort in this moment, but were the truth.

"You can see him, if you'd like." Knox gestured to the door they'd come through. "He's in the intensive care unit, but if you follow the hallway behind me, it will take you to the desk. A nurse will take you to him."

She gripped her sister's hand and stood. Then she walked past them, her head held high, her sister right beside her.

"Sorry." Miranda crossed her arms. Talking to family in this situation was a delicate game. If you couldn't make promises, you didn't talk of the future.

"It happens." Knox looked at her, his eyes saying what so many had said in the past two years.

But not normally to you.

Once, she had been the picture of perfection. Yes, behind closed doors she sometimes cried for hours. There were days where she felt more robot than person. But that robot was a better surgeon than the emotional physician who made mistakes. Who failed…

"At least the argument stopped." Knox was trying to make her feel better.

"No, it didn't. They tabled it." Knox gave her a look that made her chuckle. "I grew up with three sisters. Trust me. That argument will kick-start again as soon the crisis settles. And be renegotiated through the years."

She loved her sisters. Miranda never felt the call to motherhood, but Kelly and Olive had three each. The cousins were all around the same ages; it made family gatherings loud. If their oldest were in a car accident, the sisters would support each other and argue about fault.

"Renegotiated?"

"Yeah. If you ask Olive and Kelly about the winter of ninety-nine they will each claim it was the other's idea to go 'sledding' on the sandhill. The concussion Olive got is why her memory is fuzzy, according to Kelly. The six stitches Kelly needed to close the wound in her head, Olive's excuse." It was the way of the world amongst sisters.

"Siblings." Knox shrugged. "But are you okay?"

"You and Jackson are brothers." Miranda preferred this topic to his question. It sucked to not give patients' families too much hope. But it was necessary when the odds were still tumbling. Her slip was one others might look past, ignore as first-day jitters, but Knox knew her.

Or he had once.

"Surely the two of you have fights that get started and have to be put aside for a while?"

"No." Knox shook his head, his blue eyes staring at her in a way that made Miranda want to shift away. She wasn't the woman she'd been. And there wasn't even a good reason.

That was the thing she'd told her therapist. She'd just burned out. No catastrophic cause. No major life change. Her marriage was a disaster. Lance was cruel behind closed doors. Manipulative. A masterful gaslighter.

But she'd handled it. In fact, it was he who'd left. Saying he'd taken a new job three states over without telling her, then handing her divorce papers.

That was one thing she'd change if she got a do-over. She and Lance should not have married. A truth she'd suspected on her wedding day.

People divorced all the time. Particularly surgeons. None of the divorce stress caused her burnout.

It was like one day the switch that kept her perfect just switched off. And nothing she'd done could flip it back on.

"Miranda—"

"I'm fine." The words were spoken too fast. The defensive stance creeping through her. "Really. Just first day back. Fine. Really. Fine."

"Three fines?" The concern flipping through his blue eyes made her want to lean toward him. To confide the truth. She felt lost.

She had everything she'd wanted. A good career. Enough money in the bank to be comfortable.

Happy family time with her sisters and her new role as the fun auntie. Complaining felt wrong.

"Yep. Three fines. Just to reinforce it." She tapped her nose, offered a smile she hoped looked real, before turning and heading to the locker room. Miranda kept an ear open in case Knox said anything else.

As she entered the women's locker room, she tried to convince herself that it was all right that he didn't.

CHAPTER THREE

KNOX LOOKED OVER the interns. The fresh batch of baby doctors trying to figure out their next paths. He and Miranda had stood in a similar gaggle. That gaggle had been doctors across a wide range of specialties and across the nation for more than a decade. It was weird to feel so old and see yourself in the next group, too.

He picked out the Miranda of this group. The perfectionist already writing notes with her stylus on a tablet. A young woman stood next to her, mimicking the motions. Though she didn't look quite as determined. Had people looked at him and Miranda that way?

Picked out the two over-overachievers in a group of overachievers?

"Ready?" Miranda yawned as she stepped next to him.

"I am. Are you?" She'd disappeared after the blunder with the family yesterday. A minor misstep. Sometimes emotions got in the way when talking to family. But Miranda had always been too hard on herself.

"Yeah. I just need another cup of coffee." She held up the reusable mug and tilted her head toward the future doctors. "Ready to convince some of these kids that they want to do surgery?"

"How could they not want to!" Knox chuckled as they started toward the group. He'd joined surgical because it was the most prestigious. At least that was what the doctors who had stood where he and Miranda stood now had said. He'd stayed general rather than specializing because he liked knowing some of everything. He had his critical care certifications, and surgical oncology, and pediatrics and just about everything else, too. He worked on all sorts of cases.

"Spoken like a true surgeon." Miranda took a sip of her drink.

Her eyes were far away. Like she was looking at the interns and thinking of their time, too. But coming to a different conclusion than he did. Like maybe this wasn't the life she'd choose in a do-over.

"Good morning." Miranda raised a hand as all the interns' faces turned toward them.

Now all the tablets and styluses emerged from oversize pockets or satchels. Dutiful note takers even if they already knew this wasn't the specialty for them.

"Morning." The group's harmonized greeting made him smile.

"So who already knows surgery is for them?" Knox clapped and gave a thumbs-up to two interns on the right. The woman who'd started taking notes before they'd even walked over started to raise her hand, hesitated, then raised it fully.

Knox saw Miranda tilt her head at the hesitater. The first two hands had shot up. The third…

"Is there anyone who knows this isn't the specialty you're choosing? It's okay. Dr. Peters and I will not take it personally."

"Speak for yourself." Knox nodded before gesturing for anyone to raise their hands. "Let us know."

Three hands from the back shot up.

"Which specialty are you three looking at?"

"Pediatrics."

"Ophthalmology."

"Radiology."

"All right." Miranda smiled. "You can still ask questions. With the exception of radiology, there are surgical specialties for both."

"Some of us like to live in the dark!" The hopeful radiologist's joke let out a chorus of chuckles.

"The lights are pretty bright in surgery." Knox crossed his arms. "But what questions do you have for us?"

He and Miranda fielded the standard questions for the first twenty minutes. How to handle placements? Was it better to think of two specialties you might like in surgery? What was the best lesson to take away? Questions each class asked and surgeons and other doctors answered multiple times a year.

"How much trauma does a general surgeon see?" The question came from the hesitater.

"Quite a bit." Miranda's tone was controlled but forceful. "We are the frontline. Car accidents, ruptured appendix, fights. General surgeons see a little of everything. I am technically a general with a certification in trauma surgery and pediatric trauma care."

"And I have those and surgical oncology, and vascular surgery. And I am considering hand surgery, but most of those go to the ortho guys. All the little bones." Knox chuckled, trying to relieve the tension this question always created.

"But," Miranda added, "all specialties have great days and lows deeper than you can possibly imagine."

"Surgery seems so competitive." The woman pursed her lips as she made another note.

Knox saw the flush of the resident's cheeks and wondered if she'd meant to say it.

"Surgery is competitive no matter the specialty. General surgery is least competitive than the others and matching into it is still difficult." Miranda's answer was the textbook one. He'd read some variation on the theme on the blogs he'd searched when trying to determine his own match choices.

"Competition makes you better, though." Competition drove you to be better. It let you reach goals that you might not reach without fighting someone else for them. It was how he'd reached the point he was at.

Mostly because of the woman beside him now.

"Competition *can* be healthy."

Miranda's inflection on *can* nearly made Knox's head bounce back. They'd competed for everything; she'd won everything. It had gotten her everything.

There was no way she could regret that…right?

"Would you choose a different specialty if you could go back in time?"

That question wasn't for him. Knox found himself as interested in Miranda's answer as the young intern.

"I think the choice of specialty is an important one. If you are choosing because someone else thinks its best, or because an online post says this is the best one, or the top moneymaker, or for any reason other than it is where I feel I can spend the next thirty to forty years of my life, you open yourself up to regrets. You should make that choice for yourself, not because someone else wants it."

She hadn't answered the question. In fact, she'd fairly well avoided it. With a good speech. The interns did need to focus on things that made them happy. They'd been in school with kids who choose a career because that was what mom or dad wanted for them. That was a rough road.

Luckily for Knox—no one had wanted a say in what he did.

"Was that a yes?" The hesitater raised an eyebrow as she held the stylus. Knox would give her credit. She wanted an answer. A full answer.

"No. I would not choose a different specialty. General surgery is rewarding. The adrenaline rush of saving someone experiencing trauma is real. That isn't just a television drama moment." She took a deep breath, and the faraway look he'd seen earlier reappeared.

"But…" She looked at him then at the group of students. "I cannot look out at you and tell you there aren't changes I would make. I took a fellowship after graduating, a coveted one, that I shouldn't have. Sometimes it's easy as you compete with each other to focus on what the world says you should want, instead of what you want for yourself."

His ears buzzed and his jaw ached as he forced himself to unclench his teeth. How could she say that she'd change it? How could she acknowledge she hadn't wanted the fellowship? It was the one job he'd have taken to leave here. The one he absolutely would have said yes to.

What would his life be like if she'd realized that years ago?

"Time to start rounds." Knox cleared his throat. He needed to move, needed to push away the discomfort coating his skin. Anything to focus on something other than the what-if.

"You're very fortunate." Miranda stood next to Jill's bed. The young woman still had two tubes draining the fluid buildup in her stomach, but over all her prognosis was positive.

"He got upset sometimes, but I never thought Doug would…" Jill looked out the window. The view was a dirty roof, nothing one would actually enjoy, but she'd worked with domestic violence victims before. It wasn't the view Jill wanted; it was the avoidance. But she hadn't done anything wrong.

"It's not your fault." Miranda said words she knew Jill had heard. Shame came with the territory. It wasn't fair, only the perpetrator was responsible for intimate partner violence, but the victim always felt like they'd done something.

At least for a little while.

"When do I get to leave this floor?" Jill bit her lip before looking at Miranda. "I'd like to get out of PCU."

Progressive Care Unit or the PCU was in between the intensive care unit and a standard floor unit. The stepdown schedule for the unit varied on the severity of disease and injury. "I know you want to get off the PCU, but the fact that you aren't in ICU two days after the attack is a small miracle."

Jill brushed a tear from her cheek. "I want to go home."

"I understand. The comfort of your own bed—"

"No." Jill interrupted. "Not my own bed. Home. I moved to Phoenix for a job. For Doug's job. And then we got divorced and I stayed because…" She threw her hands in the air. "I don't know why I stayed."

"I stayed because it was easy. Until it wasn't." Miranda took a deep breath and moved to the chair by the window. If Jill wanted to look out at it, that was fine, but she wanted her to know that she was sitting opposite her.

"Are you about to tell me it's not my fault again?" Jill pinched her eyes shut. Those words were good for some people, triggers for others.

"There is no roadmap for this." Miranda barely resisted the urge to pull her legs up. "I wish there was. I wish I could give you a magic pill or something to know how to build your life around the trauma you've experienced. From before the attack and through it. Only you can figure out what that path looks like for you. But if you want to leave the city, there are programs that help you with funding if you need it. Counseling services."

"I want a fast-forward button. A way to just fast-forward six months and things be different."

"In six months, your body will be healed. Life will be different, but that doesn't mean everything will be all right. Give yourself time, Jill. You are worth it." She stood. "If you need more pain medication make sure the nurses know." Miranda planned to request a visit from the hospital counselor. Jill could always send them away. But talking to someone…

It had helped her. Once she'd finally reached out.

Lance had never raised his hands, though Miranda suspected he was capable of it. He had used emotional manipulations. Made her feel so unworthy that she pushed herself and pushed herself. Their careers were the things they focused on. Two over-overachievers. But she'd wanted an actual marriage, to come in at least second to his career goals. Unfortunately, she hadn't even been in his top ten. All slots were reserved for his career. And she thought if she just worked harder it might change.

And when she broke, when the burnout became too much for her to focus on anything, when she'd gone to administration to ask for a sabbatical, he'd called her crazy.

Denigrated his wife's mental health, using what many referred to as an ableist slur.

The worst part was that in those days she'd believed him. After achieving her entire life. Competing and winning to feel nothing when she entered the hospital. Numb to the job, her mind wandering when it needed focus. What other answer was there?

Lying in bed, depressed and feeling like she was worthless and her husband had agreed with the dark demons of depression. He'd fueled the lies her mind had told her in those days.

And she'd stayed. That rankled her far more than she wanted to admit. Then he'd left her.

Most days she still felt like an imposter. A failure hiding under a mantle of a fancy résumé and quick talking. She wanted the feeling to stop. Wanted to find a way to prove she was fine.

Knox was putting in notes at the computer workstation. He tilted his head a little as she walked up but didn't say anything. If he clenched his jaw any tighter, she worried he might pop out a few teeth.

The man had been professional today, but the relative ease they'd had yesterday seemed to evaporate this morning.

Her mind immediately jumped through their interactions, looking to see where she might have made a mistake. Then she shut the thought train down. She was not responsible for Knox's bad mood. Or if she was, that wasn't fair and not her concern. He could work through it…or not.

She'd taken on all the responsibility in her relationship with Lance. Done her best to please him. To make him happy while making herself smaller and smaller. Not happening again.

"Jill is getting restless. And she has at least another two days in PCU. Does Hope have any programs for restless patients?"

"What kind of programs?" Knox continued typing.

Miranda bit back the question, *Are you mad at me?* She was not asking that.

"Well, things like volunteers that play cards, craft materials. I had a patient that loved doing diamond paintings. Maybe a video game console to borrow, paper to write a story or letters." Each room had a television but there were only so many hours of television some could stand. Smartphones helped pass the time but they got old, too.

"Hope is not a very big hospital, Miranda."

"You don't have to tell me!" She laughed, hoping to change the direction of conversation. "Climbing the stairs here isn't as much of a workout but finding a parking spot in the garage is super easy."

"The point is," Knox said, turning toward her, "if you wanted fancy things, you should have stayed at the fancy hospital."

"Out with it." She crossed her arms. Whatever he needed to say, life would be easier for them if he let it go now.

"Excuse me?"

"No. You are not playing the fool now, Dr. Peters. You are being short with me. You've been short all day. I am asking if there is anything I can do for a patient, and you are being snarky. So, what is it you actually want to say to me?"

Knox's eyes widened and color flooded his cheeks. Embarrassment or anger, maybe a hint of both.

"You had everything. Everything. The fellowship. The fancy job. How could you not want it? How, after working so hard to beat me, could you tell an intern this morning you'd change it?" He pinched the bridge of his nose. "You got the thing

I wanted most, and you didn't even want it in the end."

Miranda blinked. She doubted Knox had meant to let all of that spill out. But now that it was here, there was no going back for either of them.

"Are you the same person you were when we were residents?" Life had changed her. Whether she wanted those changes or not was irrelevant.

"Yes." He crossed his arms. "I am still the hard-working, competitive man I was when you were last here."

Miranda looked at Knox. The muscles in his shoulders were tight and his forearms flexed. The man was tightly wound, whether he realized it or not. "Well, I had to change. I'll see you tomorrow." Then she turned and left.

What else was there to say?

CHAPTER FOUR

HE'D NOT NEEDED Jackson to tell him he'd been an ass. At least on this, Knox was self-aware. Though his brother had agreed with the analysis when he outlined what he'd said. Then helped him gather some of the things for his apology.

Knox looked at the small cabinet in the break room that had been stocked with a mishmash of things that really belonged in the trash can. He'd run Miranda's idea past Hugh via text. The head of surgery had agreed that Knox could have this cabinet.

He put a label on the cabinet and leaned back, admiring his work.

"If you lean back any farther and fall over, I will laugh before I help you up."

Miranda's light tone stunned him. He was prepared for an understandably angry morning shift.

"I'm sorry for yesterday." Knox turned, and her dark eyes met his. There were circles under them. He'd caused her to lose sleep. All because she'd changed life paths.

A pivot could be healthy. He had never pivoted, never changed paths, because this one worked.

Other people changed directions all the time. And she was back here. That was nice. Standing across from her in surgery, he'd not realized how much he'd missed her presence until she was there. And he'd screwed it all up with an overreaction!

She'd been the best candidate for the job. If it was offered today, he was sure he could come in first. But then... Then, she'd been the right choice.

"I appreciate the apology. Why are you admiring the cabinet?" Miranda's raised eyebrow made him smile.

"I stole your idea." Knox pointed to the small cabinet. It had seemed bigger when he was cleaning it out. And even with the few things he'd picked up from the store with Jackson, it was very empty.

Still, every plan had to start somewhere.

"I haven't had any ideas." Miranda crossed her arms and rolled back on her feet.

The twitch of her lips, the frown hidden not quite quick enough, stabbed through him. He'd hurt her more than he'd realized yesterday.

"Not true." Knox opened the cabinet, adding a flourish to his hand motions.

Miranda chuckled, the rich sound bringing out his own laugh.

"You look like a bad game show model. In this corner you've won an ugly living room set, but you could have chosen a nearly empty cabinet!" Miranda mimicked his motions, her smile infectious.

"It's not an empty cabinet." Knox stuck his tongue out.

"I said nearly empty," Miranda countered.

He looked at the pack of cards, diamond paintings and adult coloring books that took up almost no space and had to give her that assessment. "All right, fine, nearly empty, but I figure we can work on that."

"We?"

"Yes. You were right. We should have some options for patients that are stuck here. There is a library near the cafeteria, too. I should have remembered that yesterday. But I was too focused on…" Knox took a deep breath.

"Too focused on being angry at the past. Which is dumb. You can't be angry at the past. It's done." He laughed, but the chuckles stopped as he saw Miranda wasn't laughing.

"You are allowed to have feelings about it. You aren't allowed to take those feelings out on me." Miranda's hip buzzed.

"That sounds like something a therapist said." Knox had seen a range of counselors and therapists when he was in foster care. None of them had had much to say for a young boy who knew his family didn't want him.

They'd offered platitudes. Told him it wasn't his fault. Given him pamphlets and books. Things he was certain their textbooks said would help him.

None of it did.

What finally had was graduating close to top of his class. Getting his own place and knowing that no one would ever find him lacking again.

"I might have had a therapist say it." Miranda

shrugged as she looked at the pager. "Doesn't make it not true."

She looked up, "We have a consult down in the ER. Where is your pager?"

Knox pulled his off his hip. The battery light blinking. "Right here…and not holding a charge." It was a problem they'd had with them lately. The pagers were old but administration felt they could make do.

"I'll grab another as we head past the nurses' station." He tossed the dead weight. "I bet your other place didn't have issues with pagers."

"Parkins had issues and so did the two other hospitals I've worked at." Miranda held open the door. "Those hospitals were fancy, no way around that. But administration is the same everywhere. Cut corners to maximize profits."

Knox shook his head. "Always administration."

"The bane of all US hospitals." Miranda sighed, the frustration of a doctor who only wanted to treat patients but also had to make administration and insurance companies content. Two goals that were too often in opposition.

They walked down the flight of stairs into the ER. The buzz of the floor always reminded Knox of a well-choreographed play that dangled a little too close to full chaos. "The page said bay four."

"Dr. Peters." The young ER physician, Dr. Hinks, stepped between him and Miranda. Miranda raised a brow but stepped to the side to give them a little bit more space.

Dr. Hinks and Knox had had a few run-ins. The man believed his position as a doctor made him better than others. And he had a chip on his shoulder because he'd not matched into his chosen specialty. He'd matched into emergency medicine through the supplemental offer and acceptance program, commonly called SOAP.

That chip, and the idea that because he'd spent years in school meant his word was all that mattered, made him an incredibly difficult colleague.

His old-school belief that he shouldn't be questioned by patients, that he always knew best, was a principle most physicians were doing their best to root out. The fact that Dr. Hinks was so sure of himself despite only working in the field for a year unnerved Knox.

That level of confidence, mixed with a bitterness at the universe for not getting what you thought you were owed, could be dangerous.

"Child in bay four. Was pushed off the roof." The physician crossed his arms and shook his head. "Single mother and she wasn't home when the incident occurred. Clearly not fit to parent."

"That's quite a statement. What are you basing it on?" Miranda's question was the right one.

Which was good since Knox's head was buzzing as he saw disdain pass the physician's features.

"A feeling." Dr. Hinks rolled his eyes. "Sometimes that is all you need."

Healthcare workers saw unfortunate cases all the time. Social services was an important network to provide support to families. It was also underfunded and strained. Adding to it because of a *feeling* based on a bias was a horrid practice.

One that could have lifelong consequences.

"A feeling?" Miranda made a note on the tablet chart. "And the reason for the surgical consult?"

Dr. Hinks looked from Miranda to Knox. "She doing all the talking?"

"Excuse me?" Miranda's eyes flashed with a warning Knox doubted Dr. Hinks would take.

"I said…"

"We heard you." Knox interrupted before the physician could say anything else. "Are you planning on answering Dr. Paulson's question?"

Dr. Hinks let out a heavy sigh. As much as Knox hated getting administration involved in things, someone needed to talk to them about this man.

"He was pushed off a roof. He has a broken arm and big bruise on his side. Internal bleeding is your job."

"What's his blood pressure?" Knox checked his watch. If the kid was conscious that meant he likely wasn't hemorrhaging. The body could repair a minor internal bleed.

"Normal." Dr. Hinks shrugged.

"Normal?" Miranda's frustrated taps on the tablet mirrored Knox's thoughts. One of the main indicators of internal bleeding was low blood pressure. A large bruise might just happen with a fall. In fact, it likely *would* happen.

"When was the MRI ordered?" Knox suspected the answer but the furrow of Dr. Hinks's brows made it clear.

"Order it now." Before the man could say anything else, Knox opened the curtain and walked to bay four with Miranda, pulling it closed without waiting for Dr. Hinks.

A little boy lay on the ER bed, his mother in tears beside him, and a boy a few years older than him that had to be his big brother stood as they walked in.

"Good morning, I am Dr. Paulson." Miranda raised a hand.

"Dr. Peters." Knox nodded. "What happened?"

"I didn't mean to push him. Our cat climbed the tree and was up on the roof and…" The brother wiped a tear from his cheek.

"He told me not to follow him." The boy on the bed clenched his eyes shut and took a deep breath.

"Neither of you should have been on the roof." Their mother's stern look was softened by the tears in her eyes. This wasn't a parent who didn't care.

Knox had grown up with several of those. It was something he knew how to identify and quickly. One tiny benefit to a childhood steeped in trauma was his brain recognized it in others.

That was also one of the worst things.

"Let's start with basics." Miranda's voice was calm. "I'm Dr. Paulson, what is your name?" Miranda looked at the boy on the bed with the air cast on his right arm.

"Leo." He frowned. "It's my cat. Sprinkles is my responsibility. If I hadn't left my window open."

"Blame games don't help anyone right now. You can spend years pointing fingers at each other." Miranda waved a finger.

Was that what happened with her sisters? He and Jackson weren't bound by early-childhood memories. Just teenage years trying to break the cycle they'd been thrown into. Two young men bent on proving everyone wrong.

"When you fell, you tried to catch yourself?" Miranda gestured to the air cast.

He needed a real cast. But the priority was the MRI, even though, based on the steady blood pressure reading on the monitor in the corner, the child's coloring and the fact that he seemed completely lucid, Knox figured it would come back clear.

"I did."

"And the bruise." Miranda moved as Leo used his left hand to lift his shirt.

Knox shook his head. "That is a shoe print."

"Yep." Leo glared at his brother. "Sprinkles, my cat."

Knox could have guessed that by the name.

"She scratched Ben and he kicked me. Next

thing I knew I was on the ground, my right arm screaming in pain."

"If you'd stayed inside…" Ben crossed his arms, but the tears in his eyes made it clear this was an accident.

"Well," Miranda said, looking at Knox, "I think Dr. Hinks was being overly cautious."

Knox nodded. Miranda's diplomacy was far better than the thoughts running through his head.

"So he doesn't need the MRI?" Leo's mom looked at her son, her bottom lip trembling as she ran her hand over his dark hair.

"I think we should still run it," Knox stated. "Dr. Hinks already put the order in. That bruise is nasty-looking. Based on Leo's vitals, I don't think we will find a bleed, but if it is slow, you could be back here in a few hours or days. And that adds complications."

"Right." His mother leaned over, kissing Leo's head. "That makes sense."

She hadn't wanted to challenge them, but Knox could see the relief in her face. She wanted to make sure Leo was fine, other than the broken arm.

Miranda tapped out a few things on her tablet. "If it comes back clear, Dr. Peters and I won't see you again, Leo."

Leo wiped a tear from his cheek. "At least I get a fancy cast." He pointed to the wall where there was a display of cast colors.

"I broke my ankle when I was about your age.

What I wouldn't have given for a blue sparkle cast. Choose well, because you will have it for weeks." Miranda smiled, then turned to Knox. "Anything else, Dr. Peters?"

"I never broke any bones, but I would caution against the yellow—it gets dirty-looking fast." He gave Leo a thumbs-up. "Unless the grungy look is what you are going for."

"Ma'am—" Knox looked at Leo's mother "—can we talk to you for a minute in the hall?"

Leo's mother looked at her boys, her features falling.

"Just the hall, promise." Knox could see the worry. "If Leo or Ben need anything, you'll hear them."

She kissed Leo again, offered a watery smile to Ben and then led the way out of the room.

Miranda closed the curtain, and Knox turned his attention to Leo's mother. The woman's shoulders were straight. Tears coated her eyes but her lips were set. A woman ready for battle.

That confirmed that Dr. Hinks had said something unsavory.

"I am a fit mother." Her voice wavered. "I am also a single mother. We are in the twenty-first century. I will not be treated like some pariah because my ex-husband wants nothing to do with the family he helped create."

He saw Miranda's head turn out of the corner

of his eye, but Knox didn't break eye contact with the boys' mother.

"I am not doubting that." Knox held up his hands. "Let's start at the beginning. I am Knox, this is Miranda." Titles were fine, but they could put some people on edge, particularly if they'd been weaponized.

"Stacy."

"It's nice to meet you, Stacy. The main reason I wanted to talk was about Ben."

"He didn't mean to kick his brother. He was trying to get the cat…who would have jumped off the roof and been fine." Stacy sucked in a sob. "I swear, they are good boys."

"Of course they are." Knox shook his head. "But I think Ben might do well to talk to one of our counselors while you wait for the MRI and its results. He's upset, which is understandable. But having him talk to someone who can reinforce that this was an accident may help."

Kids internalized a lot more than adults often realized. Ben was worried. He'd wanted to do the right thing for his pet and now his brother was waiting to find out if he had internal bleeding. None of that was the plan, but the rethinking, the rehashing, the wondering how you might have changed the outcome. It could stay with a kid for years.

Particularly if his and Miranda's initial assumption about Leo not needing surgery was wrong.

"We can put in the request for the counselor."

"Okay." Stacy looked to the closed curtain. "That might be good. But you said main reason. What else?"

Knox looked behind him, no sign of the other reason he wanted to discuss. He leaned against the wall, his hand falling in line with a poster most people ignored.

"I wanted to make sure you knew what all Leo's rights are as a patient." His hand tapped the line he was drawing Stacy's attention to. Miranda's smile was so big, he thought her teeth might radiate down the hall. This was important, but if admin asked, he could also say he hadn't technically recommended it.

Her mouth opened, then shut. "I can get Leo a new doctor. But I like you and Dr. Paulson."

"We aren't Leo's physicians of record. Dr. Hinks is." Miranda's tone was controlled, but he saw the twitch in the corner of her eye. Miranda wasn't impressed by the man, either.

"So if I wanted another doctor for Leo, I can ask?"

"Yes." Knox tapped the printout on the wall one more time before standing. The patients' rights poster was required to be prominently displayed. It clearly outlined her entitlement to choose a new physician, if there was an issue.

It wasn't talked about much, but it was state law.

Administration could be difficult, but with Miranda and Knox backing her, they'd make the change. Better that than a lawsuit. "Mention it to one of the nurses and let them know they can talk to me or Dr. Paulson, if they have questions."

"Thank you." Stacy closed her eyes, a little of the worry decreasing from her cheeks.

Stacy moved past him, and Knox clenched his fists. The emotional drain of dealing with abuse situations was terrible, but threatening a mother when it was clear an accident had occurred was also wrong. A power play from a man who wanted to prove he had more power than others.

"Knox?"

Miranda's dark eyes were trained on him, kindness, and he feared pity, clear in them. He couldn't explain the blend of emotions rocketing through him. He'd been the one without power for his entire childhood. Watched bullies, kids and adults pick on him because he had less power than them. That a health professional would do the same...

He'd not solved problems with his fists since grade school. But the urge was there. "I need to get some air. I'll catch up with you."

Knox walked past Miranda without looking back. He needed a breather. In a few minutes he could put back the feelings of unworthiness, the memories of having to deal with an unfair system, the hurts he kept buried—unless he was using them to push himself forward.

* * *

Miranda grabbed an adult coloring book and the crayons. The owls and flowers would take a while to color. It would give Jill something to do.

The gesture from Knox was sweet. An acknowledgment that he'd messed up. An apology with thought behind it. Her parents never apologized, and the few her ex-husband delivered had been tinged with insinuations that it was Miranda who should apologize.

"Dr. Paulson." Leah, the charge nurse on Med-Surg, passed her the tablet chart. "The MRI results are back and Dr. Hinks is at the nurses' station. He's looking for Dr. Peters."

"Dr. Peters is removing an appendix." Miranda had seen the twenty-something male come in. Dragged by his roommate, who told him that his pride would kill him. It would have, too. The appendix had ruptured. If left untreated the man had only a day or so left in the mortal plane.

Knox had been out of sorts since the ER consult. An appendectomy, even one that had ruptured, was basically routine for a general surgeon. Knox had jumped at the opportunity for the surgery. Looking for a reason to let his mind focus on anything other than the issues Dr. Hinks had raised before.

She knew that need. Knew the desire to focus on healing someone else. But was he letting himself heal?

Easier said than done—she knew that, too.

"I know. I was hoping you might be able to defuse him." Leah looked over her shoulder. "Dr. Peters doesn't deserve to be yelled at by Dr. Hinks."

"And I do?" Miranda winked, making sure the nurse understood that Miranda was kidding. "Let me run this to Jill—"

"I can do that." Leah held out her hands. The unspoken *Dr. Hinks needs to be gone now.*

Miranda handed the nurse the coloring supplies. "Ask Jill what else she might like. I'm going to talk to administration about getting a few more things. I'd like to get things people want."

Leah nodded as she headed out.

Miranda pulled up Leo's results. Knox was right. The bruise was deep but there were no signs of internal bleeding. He'd enjoy hearing that when he was out of surgery.

Closing her eyes she took a deep breath, then opened her eyes and straightened her shoulders. Walking out the door, she mentally planned her speech.

Most physicians were inherently good people. They went into the profession because they wanted to heal the sick and injured. A small handful were in it for the money—not the reason she'd choose, but she understood it. A tiny fraction were here for power.

Because knowledge of the healing arts made them feel superior. Those doctors were dangerous, and even with only a few minutes of interaction, she knew Dr. Hinks fell into this category.

"Dr. Hinks, I just checked the results of the MRI. Good news. No internal bleeding." Miranda offered a smile she knew he didn't want. But in her experience playing extra nice with these types often made them uncomfortable.

They thrived on terror. And she refused to play into that desire.

"I am *here* to talk to Dr. Peters." He crossed his arms and looked behind her. "Where is he?"

"In surgery." Miranda kept her smile in place. At least her marriage had trained her not to respond in these situations. "The MRI showed no sign of bleeding. There is nothing you need to discuss with Dr. Peters you can't discuss with me."

"I want to discuss why he told the patient's mother to request a new doctor."

The root of the issue. Dr. Hinks didn't care about Leo. Or his mother's situation. Or his brother's guilt. It was about his image.

"I was there. Knox did not tell her to request a new doctor."

"Then tell me why she did." Color flooded Dr. Hinks's face.

Miranda's stomach tumbled but she didn't flinch. He was trying to intimidate her. It wasn't going to work.

"She has the right to request a new doctor if something isn't working. It is her right as a minor patient's mother." Miranda kept her tone level; Lance had used any inflection of emotion against her.

Calling her reactions crazy. A term used to demonize those with mental health issues since its invention. The only good to come from that relationship was her ability to deal with bullies and abusers. Dr. Hinks certainly fell into the first category, and it was possible he fell into the second, too.

"She is just mad because I said she was unfit."

Gee. How would that make her angry?

"Accidents happen, Dr. Hinks. That is the way with children. And for what it's worth, parents who've hurt their children, or who don't care about them, do not bring them to the emergency room until it's almost too late." It was something her mentor had told her as a first-year medical student.

"Social services can clear her, if there is nothing there." Dr. Hinks crossed his arms. "And I made sure the social worker knew she'd requested transfer after I suggested there was a problem."

"Clear her!" Knox's voice was tight as he stepped to Miranda's side.

He still wore his surgical cap. "Clear her? Do you know how overworked caseworkers are? Do you know what filling the system with biased reports because you have an agenda does? Do you know the trauma of foster care? Even when it is in the best interest of the children, it is trauma."

"Knox." Miranda didn't realize a body could

be that rigid. His neck muscles were tight, his jaw was clenched and his fingers were digging into his arms as he stared down Dr. Hinks.

He ignored her soft words. "If you look at your patients this way, maybe you shouldn't be seeing them."

"Is that a threat?" Dr. Hinks looked like he hoped it was. A bead of fear pressed at her neck. This man was dangerous to more than just patients.

Miranda stepped between the two men. "I think it's time we take a breather. Tensions are high and our jobs stressful. Leo is all right. That is what's most important. Right?"

Knox nodded. Dr. Hinks didn't respond.

"This isn't over." Dr. Hinks pointed a finger at Knox. "Tell another patient of mine to request transfer and I *will* speak to the board about you."

He turned on his heel and stormed out of the Med-Surg bay.

"Knox?"

He stood there, his eyes focused on the closed door where Dr. Hinks had disappeared. "I'm fine."

"I might believe that, if your jugular vein wasn't visibly pulsating on your neck."

Knox didn't look at her. He just took a deep breath. "I need to talk to Julio's roommate. Infection was spreading from the rupture. He'll be here a few days. And his roommate is listed as his emergency contact."

"Good thing he came in, then."

"Yep." Knox blew out a heavy breath then walked through the same doors that Dr. Hinks had gone through a few minutes ago.

CHAPTER FIVE

"GOOD MORNING, KNOX." Miranda waved as they walked from the garage to the elevator.

"Morning." His tone was soft and there were circles under his eyes. So today did not herald the return of the fun Knox.

That was fine. She understood. Though she wasn't sure why the argument with Dr. Hinks last week was still weighing on him.

"Are you getting any rest?" It was a question she wished people had asked her when she was in the final stages of work before burnout stole her ability to function. People often only saw the productivity, not the pain or worry behind it.

"Enough."

Miranda tilted her head as the elevator doors opened. "Enough rest or—" she lowered her voice, trying to sound silly, while expressing concern "—enough...stop talking to me?"

Knox's blue eyes widened and he smiled. The first she'd seen since the argument with Dr. Hinks.

Was it weird that she was tracking his smiles? That was a question she might want to investigate another time.

"Is that supposed to be a cartoon villain sound, Miranda?"

"No. Although maybe it fits. I didn't watch cartoons growing up. Did I do it right?" This wasn't the conversation she'd planned to have with him. Or anyone ever. But he was finally giving more than one-word answers, and she'd take whatever topic made that happen.

"You didn't watch cartoons growing up? What did you do?"

"Study." She shrugged. The only television in her house was in her parents' room. They did not permit their children to "waste" time in such a way. And once the girls had gotten laptops, they'd installed spyware on the computers under the guise of keeping them safe.

Control was what her therapist called it. Miranda had to agree, though she still wondered if they hadn't pressured her to be her best if she'd be standing where she was now.

"Seriously, Miranda. What did you do for fun?"

"Math games." She saw the same look she'd seen so often from friends when she mentioned how she was raised. It was weird what you could find normal, if you didn't know anything else.

"But we aren't discussing my childhood." She winked as the elevator doors opened. "We are talking about if you got enough rest."

Knox looked away as they started toward the locker room.

"Knox, what is it about Dr. Hinks that has thrown you so far off?" The man was an ass. A certified bully who clearly liked his position of power over his patients. That was terrible; sadly, he wasn't the only doctor she'd met who felt that way.

Hell, she'd been married to one.

"Did you know he is the CEO's nephew?"

"No. But that doesn't surprise me." Nepotism was a part of nearly every professional organization, unfortunately. "His comment on speaking to the board was pretty telling."

"What do you mean?" Knox leaned against the wall, his face finally free of some of the stress she'd seen there over the past week.

Man, even tired and stressed the man was hot as hell.

"Would you ever threaten to talk to the board?" Miranda knew the answer. Knox might talk to admin, or Dr. Lawton if there were problems, but only a very specific kind of person threatened to go to a hospital board.

"Of course not."

"That's because of who you are." Miranda tapped his shoulder and felt her eyes widen at the contact. The touch had been instinctual but the fire of need it brought made her clear her throat. Knox was hurting; she was offering comfort. That was all.

Or at least that should be all.

"And his reaction is all about him." Knox looked at the spot where her fingers had lain just a minute ago. "Easier to drop if he wasn't so bent on hurting patients he thought were less than him."

"Agreed." Miranda shook her head. Unfortunately, she wasn't sure there was anything they could do about that, other than ensure if anyone asked about Stacy, Leo and Ben that they were honest. The boys were fine. All indications were that it was an accident.

"Hey, you two! Hanging in the hallway. It's a fun pastime." Jackson's grin was huge as he slapped Knox on the shoulder. "Good to see you not just grumpy facing everywhere. Thanks for that, Miranda."

"Not sure I had anything to do with it." Though if she did, she wouldn't mind. Making Knox smile was oddly rewarding.

"It's tots night at Mulligan's, we going?" Jackson was nearly bouncing. "I'll even let you play darts."

"You realize that you can get tots at the store and just use the air fryer, right?" Knox laughed, "But I will take you up on the offer of darts. Want to join us?"

Knox's blue eyes held hers. A look in them Miranda wanted to believe was something other than surprise that he'd asked her.

"What is tots night?"

"Now you've done it." Knox shook his head. "You should come, but I am going to change into scrubs to avoid listening to Jackson wax poetically about his favorite bar night."

"It's amazing." Jackson waved at the departing

Knox, clearly unconcerned about his statement regarding whatever tots night was.

"We're talking about tater puffs. The little fried pieces of potato that you serve school children?" Somehow it felt like this should be some kind of euphemism, but for what, she couldn't even hazard a guess.

"Yes!" Jackson clapped. "Mulligan's hosts it once a month. It's all you can eat tots for five dollars. Tots and beer. It's the best."

"Is it?"

"Yes." Jackson shook his head. "And that doubt I hear just confirms what I already know. You need to come. Once you experience tots night, there is no going back."

"All right. Sure." It was silly and something she'd never usually do, but Jackson seemed so invested. And it wasn't like there was much in her schedule to keep her away.

Jackson clapped. He legitimately clapped.

"Wow. You are passionate about tots."

"Yep. And Knox is passionate about darts. You should play a round with him. But be advised, he always wins."

"Does he?" Miranda looked to the closed door where Knox had disappeared a few minutes ago. "Well, maybe I will give him a run for his money."

"Tell me you are secretly great at darts." Jackson's eyes widened, the hope in them shocking.

"I might be." Miranda winked. She hadn't lied

to Knox. She did study and do math rather than play or watch television like most kids. However, her parents had allowed the girls to play pool to demonstrate geometry and physics components and darts for adding and subtracting, and hand-eye coordination.

Skills the girls could use, rather than just fun pastimes.

"Tonight. Mulligan's Tot Night. You will be there."

"Sure, Jackson. I'll be there."

"You know she probably isn't going to show up." Knox took a small swig of the beer before him as he looked at the door. The door where Miranda had yet to walk through.

"Funny. I'm not the one watching that door like a hawk." Jackson slapped him on the back before grabbing another tot.

His brother only ate the potato variants at Mulligan's. The one time Knox purchased an actual bag of them and fried them at the house, Jackson hadn't even tried one.

He wasn't wrong about the door watching, though. Knox had watched the front door from the moment he'd walked in here. Jackson swore Miranda planned to come, but he couldn't quite believe she might show up.

Miranda belonged someplace much finer than Mulligan's.

Which is why when the door opened and she walked in wearing a yellow sundress and low heels, he nearly went to his knees with desire. She stood out in most places but, dressed as a literal breath of fresh air in a dive bar, damn.

"Your mouth is hanging open, Knox." Miranda gave him a playful nudge on the shoulder as she moved between him and Jackson. "These the famous tots? Can I steal one or do I have to buy my own, Jackson?"

She'd leaned against the bar, her tan legs brushing his. She'd called him out, and she'd not been wrong. Miranda looked lovely any day. But with her curly hair down, in the sundress that hugged her in all the right places, she was mouthwatering. And he was far from the only one in this joint to realize it.

"You can steal one. But only one." Jackson chuckled, "Then you have to buy your own. At five dollars for all you can eat, they are a steal."

Miranda looked at Knox and shook her head. "I thought he was kidding about the tots. He really meant just plain tater puffs."

Knox leaned a little closer, the scent of lemon and sugar wrapping through him. Of course she smelled as good as she looked. "He never kids about the tots."

Miranda took one and popped it into her mouth. Her eyes showed what Knox expected. It was just a fried potato. His brother loved them, but most people were here because it was a cheap beer and bar food night. Not because there was something heavenly about the tots.

"It's good." Miranda looked at Jackson, and Knox saw his brother shake his head before walking off to talk to one of the paramedics from the hospital.

"Did I upset him?" Miranda leaned past Knox to get a better view of the beers on tap.

"He loves the tots here. I find them over oily but don't tell him I told you that. I can't deal with the drama it might cause." Knox put a hand over his heart, enjoying the smile lighting up Miranda's eyes.

"Can I get the cider please?" Miranda started to hand her card to the bartender but he waved it away.

"Wha—?"

"Jackson paid for your first drink about ten minutes ago." The heat rushed to Knox's face as he tried and failed to clear his throat.

"Jackson?"

Was that a twinge of sadness he heard? Or was he imagining the slight downward tilt of her lips?

"Yeah. He said I was watching the door too much. I told him you probably weren't coming and he bet me you would by buying your drink."

What he did not add was that Jackson told Bill, the bartender, the first drink for the woman that made Knox swoon was on him.

The blush in Miranda's cheeks as she took a sip of her cider made his insides rush. She truly was the definition of gorgeous!

"I thought you promised me a game of darts." Miranda's hand brushed his shoulder as she slid off the stool. "I bet I can give you a run for your money."

He doubted that, but he wanted her to try. "I will never turn down a round of darts."

"All right." Miranda handed him his darts; her fingers touched his hands for a millisecond but it burned. The small crush he'd had on her when they were interns was roaring back and he didn't quite know how to put it back in the mental cage he'd forgotten about until she'd returned.

Or nearly forgotten about. One did not forget Miranda Paulson.

"You want to go first or me?" Miranda held up a dart, looking at the board like a pro.

"Go for it." Knox stood and watched as her dart landed dead center in the bull's-eye.

Her eyes were bright as she grinned. "Your turn."

Was that a lucky break? No. He didn't think so. The hustler in him, the kid who had grown up taking so many adults for their cash at this game, knew when he met another. If he was still playing for coin, Knox would toss this game and walk.

But they weren't competing for anything more

than bragging rights—and for the first time in forever someone might actually beat him.

Knox tossed the dart. Bull's-eye.

Miranda stepped up to the line. Bull's-eye.

They repeated the pattern for all three throws. And the next three and the next three.

"Someone is finally keeping up with Knox!" He wasn't sure who'd called it out but he saw Miranda smile as she stood beside him.

He'd beaten every one of the regulars, and the gathered crowd was enjoying this almost as much as he was.

"It's your turn, Knox." Miranda's voice was soft and her hip brushed his.

"Trying to distract me?" Knox raised a brow as he raised the dart. He threw it without looking—bull's-eye.

"If I was, it doesn't seem to be working." She winked, holding his gaze as she raised her dart and threw it the same way he had. Bull's-eye.

"All right. Now they are just showing off."

The comment buzzed around him, but Knox didn't take his eyes off her.

"Are we just showing off?" Her dark gaze was a rush he'd not experienced in so long. "Your turn."

He dared not take his gaze from hers, fear that this moment, whatever it was, would vanish if he blinked. Raising his final dart, he tossed it. He knew it was close to the bull's-eye but not a direct hit.

She raised her hand and let her final dart fly. He knew from the crowd's cheer that it hit dead center. Miranda Paulson won.

He'd come in second to her, just like he always had. And Knox couldn't care less.

Her lips. Her full, kissable, perfect lips were so close. The urge to dip his head, to chase whatever heady connection was pulling through them, was almost overwhelming.

Before Knox could give in to the moment, Jackson's hands slapped his back. "That was the best thing ever!"

"Even better than the tots?" Miranda high-fived Jackson but her gaze didn't leave Knox.

"Even better than the tots."

"Best two of three?" Knox raised a brow.

She stepped a little closer. "Think you can beat me?" The last shot had been luck. Her hands had shaken so badly as she stared at Knox's mouth. She'd let it loose just to end the game. When the crowd cheered, she'd known she'd won, but her eyes had refused to abandon the man before her.

"Scared the first time was a fluke?" His eyes glittered with the challenge.

Miranda stepped a little closer, lifting just a little on her toes. "You might regret challenging me." She whispered the words, enjoying the flush of color on his neck.

She was flirting with Knox Peters. It wasn't the

plan for tonight. Or maybe it was. Miranda had picked the sundress and heels, knowing she'd be out of place but wanting to see the look on Knox's face.

And she'd not been disappointed. The man's mouth had literally hung to the floor. She'd meant to make a joke. She thought she had, but the funny jaunt she'd designed to make them laugh had escaped her.

No. When she'd seen his face, Miranda had almost swooned herself.

"I will never regret challenging you."

Wow. She didn't know what to say to that. "I'm going to get a drink." Miranda stepped back. She needed a moment. And something cold to chill the heat pouring through her.

Sliding up to the bar, she waved for the bartender. Knox joined her almost immediately.

"Drinks are on me."

"Only—"

Knox held up a hand. "It's a standing rule that the loser pays."

Loser pays. Of course. She'd almost joked that he could only buy it if this was a date. The words hadn't tumbled out before he cleared the actual reason. Of course it was just a dart rule.

Miranda might have the hots for the doc but Knox was just keeping up with rules.

"Another cider or do you want a fancy drink since it's on me?"

Miranda leaned her head against her hand, careful to make sure they didn't touch against the crowded bar while they waited for the bartender. "Does this place have fancy drinks?"

Knox's chuckle lit up her soul. "I mean, they can make some cocktails that they will charge you an arm and a leg for."

"Technically, they'd be charging you an arm and a leg. Since I won and all." Miranda winked. She'd never bragged about winning. The win wasn't the main goal, after all. Her entire life, she'd tried to come in first to earn her parents' love. And no amount of winning had ever achieved that.

Not that they would have cared about winning a dart game in a dive bar. Still, the challenge felt nice as she nearly leaned toward Knox.

Knox laid a hand over his heart, leaning back just a hint, in playful hurt. "You were victorious, but next time it shall be me."

She opened her mouth to respond, but before she could a drunk white man pushed into her. The distance she'd kept between her and Knox evaporated and his arm went protectively around her waist. Heat molded through her, and she bit the inside of her lip to keep her sigh contained.

"Watch it!" Knox held up his free hand, not pushing the drunk but making sure he didn't come closer to Miranda.

Protection wasn't something she needed, but Miranda couldn't deny how nice it felt.

"It's getting a little rowdy." Miranda looked around. As much as she wanted to stay with Knox, she had no desire to see a repeat of the night they reunited.

Knox looked down the bar, disappointment clear on his face. "It isn't usually like this, but you're right." He raised his free hand to wave to Jackson.

It was only then that Miranda registered his other arm was still wrapped around her waist. She should pull back, but the drunk was still right next to her, waving at the overloaded barkeep. It was a good excuse to stay exactly where she was.

"This is a little much." Jackson's voice was risen, and if he thought anything of her in Knox's arms he didn't say it. "Even for tots night."

"I'm going to walk Miranda to her car. See if you can close out our tabs." Knox shifted her away from the bar.

She waved at Jackson. "Thanks for the invite."

Jackson's dark eyes focused on Knox's arm around her waist before meeting her gaze. "Anytime, Miranda. Watching you beat him at darts might be this year's highlight."

"I hope not. There is still a lot of year left." Miranda waved, then let Knox guide her through the crowd.

"Where did you park?" Knox's hand dropped from her waist as soon as they cleared the front door.

It was the right choice. They were out of the

crowd, but she wished he'd kept it there. Wished there were a reason to keep it there.

"Parking lot two streets over." She looked at him then started toward her car. Silence dragging between them.

As they got close to the second street, the flashing lights of emergency vehicles came into view. A bouncer was talking to several uniformed police officers.

"Guess that explains why Mulligan's was overcrowded." Knox stuffed his hands in his pockets. "This is a college bar. Doesn't matter the night, it's always packed."

"Oh." Miranda didn't know what else to say. She hadn't spent any time at bars in college. In fact, even with her trip to Mulligan's this evening she wouldn't need all her fingers to count the number of bars she'd been in.

"You didn't visit college bars, did you?"

"That obvious?" Miranda laughed as she shook her head. "I swear there must be a sign around my neck that screams I'm not fun."

Knox reached for her hand. "I did not say that!"

"No. I did." Miranda shrugged. How many times had Lance told her she wasn't fun? That she didn't know how to have fun? Of course his idea of fun was schmoozing with colleagues who might help his climb up the career ladder.

"Miranda—"

"It's not a big deal, Knox. Did you spend a lot of

time in college bars?" She could see him dancing with college girls. Enjoying himself but also making sure everyone got home on time and safely.

"Yes, but I was behind the bar." He said the words with such coolness.

She'd known several people who worked their way through school that way. "I had a job at lab."

"That does not surprise me. Were you doing tests and running scans?"

"No." Miranda pointed to her car. "I followed the cleaning staff, construction workers and anyone else who wasn't an employee." She saw the surprise on his face and understood. It was a weird job, one she'd found out about from a friend of a friend's dad.

"I guess they did work for the Department of Defense or one of the national labs or something. I had to have a security clearance but I have no idea what the actual place did. The job let me study while getting paid."

"Nice."

"This is me." She leaned against her car, not quite ready to say goodbye. "Thanks for walking me to the car."

"No problem." Knox started to lean toward her. For the briefest second she thought he might kiss her. Then he shifted and looked over his shoulder. "I should get back to Jackson. I'll see you at the hospital on Thursday. Enjoy your day off."

"Thanks." Her cheeks were hot. Thank goodness the dark parking lot hid the color seeping through her cheeks. Of course Knox wasn't planning to kiss her.

She'd beaten him at darts and had a fun night with colleagues. That should be enough.

CHAPTER SIX

THE SUN WAS barely over the horizon as Knox pounded the pavement. He'd gone three miles already and still hadn't driven thoughts of Miranda from his mind. Her lips, the pink full lips that had haunted his dreams, flashed in his memory. He'd nearly leaned in to kiss her last night.

It had felt so natural. Like what he was supposed to do. But they weren't on a date. He was simply walking her to her car. A friend looking after a friend.

He looked at his phone, pushing the button to change the song. He needed something faster. Something strong to drown out his thoughts. Knox briefly considered raising the volume but he was already getting a warning from his smart watch that he was over his recommended volume usage for the week.

Knox sucked in a deep breath, letting the burn in his lungs and limbs be his focus. It nearly worked, until he caught sight of the runner coming down the path.

Miranda.

She was in black Spandex and bright yellow sports bra with pink headphones on her ears. Delectable did not even begin to cover the descriptor. Brilliant and beautiful.

"Knox." Miranda blew out a breath and pulled her left leg behind her, stretching while stopped on the path by him. "Out for a run, too?"

He pulled the earbud from his ear, his mind doing its best to focus all his attention on her face. She was stunning, and her smile was intoxicating. She did not deserve to be ogled when out for exercise.

"Yeah. I just finished three miles. You still going?"

"I still have a chapter left before I call it quits." Miranda tapped the headphones around her neck.

"Chapter?" The question slipped out even though it shouldn't shock him that Miranda listened to books while working out. Did she ever just have fun?

She pulled her other leg up, her eyes looking away from him. "Just a book I downloaded from the library."

"Any good?" He never listened to books or podcasts while working out. He needed music, something with a heavy beat, otherwise he had no interest in moving. But he enjoyed audiobooks for when he was cleaning or just hanging about his condo.

"Yeah. It's fine." Miranda cleared her throat.

"What's the title? I'm looking for something new to add to my library." He enjoyed science fiction, fantasy and the occasional romance novel.

Anything that let him leave the world of trauma he often worked in.

"From Lazy to Nearly Perfect."

"Lazy. Who do you know that's lazy?" Knox chuckled then caught it. "Miranda."

"That was my buzzer. I need to keep my pace up." She put the headphones back on and darted off.

He waited until she was around the corner before closing his eyes and mentally kicking himself. Damn it. How did he manage to say the wrong thing around her so often?

Knox looked at his watch. He'd done more than he'd planned this morning. It was time for a shower and then a coffee at the shop on the corner of his and Jackson's condos. They'd lived together from the time they were teens. Rented out Jackson's condo for years. Then when the adjoining unit went up for sale, Knox had bought it. Jackson owned his now, too.

He ran to his door, not surprised to see no sign of life in Jackson's windows. The man said he'd earned the right to sleep in. He wasn't wrong, but Knox had never managed to stay in bed past six.

Knox did a few stretches then jumped in the shower. His mind going back to Miranda—listening to a self-help book while running. Who did that?

Miranda Paulson. That was who.

But lazy. That was not a descriptor that could be placed on her. Ever!

I failed...

Her words from that first night pummeled against his chest. What had happened on the East Coast? There were no answers today, but Knox was going to find a way to figure it out.

He dressed, walked out the front door, enjoying the fresh morning air. Now to add caffeine to his already pulsing blood. Maybe some people-watching would let him get Miranda out of his mind.

Pulling open the coffee shop door, Knox took a deep breath. Roasted beans were one of his favorite scents.

"You're blocking the door, Dr. Peters. Always risky at a coffee shop."

"Miranda." Knox grinned. Clearly, the universe planned for them to spend time together today. Who was he to question that on the second unexpected encounter?

"Fancy seeing you here." She had a large bag with a giant book sticking out. This one titled *Working on Yourself: Find the "You" You Were Meant to Be.* She certainly had a reading niche going.

Knox stepped to the side to let her pass. "Funny isn't it. Let me get your coffee."

"Knox, you don't need."

"Do I or do I not owe you a drink for losing at darts last night?"

Miranda shook her head. "I wasn't planning on calling that debt in." She leaned toward him then seemed to catch herself. "Besides, I think my coffee might be more expensive than a beer."

"Miranda Paulson drinks fancy coffee!" Knox crossed his arms to keep himself from playfully nudging her shoulder. "I had you pegged as a black coffee drinker."

She made a face, sticking her tongue out and shuddering. "Absolutely not!"

"I happen to enjoy a black coffee." Knox stuck his own tongue out, mimicking her.

"And I am happy for you. I want cream and sugar and sometimes even whipped cream on top. If you plan to *judge* me on that, then, oh, well."

Her emphasis on the word bothered him. "You get what you want, but I am buying. Who knows when I can convince you to come to Mulligan's again." Last night was not the bar's best showing. Add that to the disaster before…

At least it looked like they visited the same coffee house. Seeing Miranda outside the hospital was a gift Knox didn't feel like giving up.

She ordered a fancy Frappuccino, with whipped topping, her eyes daring him to say something. All he did was order his regular and pay. Her shoulders relaxed a little and he wondered who would say something about a coffee order that might make her so defensive.

"I'm going to get a table. Want to join me?"

His plans to head home, curl up on his couch and watch old game shows disappeared in an instant. "As long as I won't be interrupting your reading?"

Miranda's hand moved to the book as she shook her head. "Nope. I've already read it. Just looking over some of the notes I made in the margins."

Knox opened his mouth but no words materialized. Notes in the margins… He read medical journals and made notes. The field moved too quickly to throw away learning when you finally earned the title of doctor. But his own free time never included note taking.

And that's why she beat you at everything.

She waited a moment longer then wandered to a table in the corner. Knox turned, waiting for their coffees. Her frilly one with whipped topping and caramel drizzle was a work of art. Was this the one extravagance she let herself have?

Surely not.

"One caramel mocha frap!" Knox handed her the drink as he sipped his own.

Miranda's fingers brushed his as she took the plastic cup; a delicate rose flowing into her cheeks. Maybe she was as interested in him as he was her.

"All right, why the self-help books, Miranda? You are one of the most accomplished people I know. What else could you possibly hope to achieve?" He made sure the grin on his face was genuine. If she didn't answer, he'd drop it. Talk about other things or just sit quietly with her in the corner.

"It's nice that you think that." Miranda bit her lip, then took a deep sip of her drink. "It's not true, though."

"It's not?" He didn't believe that for a second, but it was clear in the downturn of her lips, the far-off look in her eyes and the small slump in her shoulders that she believed it.

The world had beaten her down. He'd been that person once. The kid no one believed in. The fact that people had done the same to Miranda... Knox took a deep breath, letting the smell of roasted beans calm him. Going on a campaign of rage at the injustices of the world wouldn't solve anything.

And it wouldn't help Miranda.

"I burned out. I know I said that, but I mean I really burned out. I had days I couldn't even get out of bed." Miranda's fingers fidgeted on the table, drawing little patterns as she refused to look at him.

"That doesn't sound like burnout."

"Sounds like failure, right? That's what Lance said." The monotone words were knives. Only someone who'd been told that repeatedly—and believed it—could say it so blithely.

Now his fury had a target. Her husband, the man who'd sworn vows for better or worse, had said such a horrible thing.

"It sounds like clinical depression, Miranda."

He fought the urge to point out that she was a doctor, a surgeon; she knew the signs. And so had her ex-husband.

Around thirty percent of individuals developed depression post-surgery. Surgeons and counselors were trained to remind patients that the isolation and edema caused during recovery were temporary. The good news was most patients' depression resolved within months of surgery.

"My life was good, though. What did I have to be depressed about?"

"Did Lance say that?" Knox took a drink of his coffee to keep from balling up his fists.

Miranda shrugged. "He might have mentioned it. I know that he was an ass. My counselor helped with that after the divorce. I know I was depressed. I know it's a serotonin issue. I understand that, but it was more than that."

She blew out a breath. There was more on the tip of her tongue, but she seemed to have run out of words.

The mood around the table was far too tight. Leaning across, he made a silly face. "I read one self-help book. It was all about keeping lists and staying organized. I mostly remember the raised lettering on the cover. It felt nice." Knox shook his head, horror at the memory of trying to read it returning. It had been recommended by one of his teachers, a way to focus his tasks.

She'd meant well. One of the few adults in his

young life who saw through the mad-at-the-world kid to the well of potential beneath it. *If* he turned in his assignments.

If it was surgery or medical knowledge, he kept everything locked in. If it was something else, there was a good chance that he'd forget. Thank goodness for auto bill pay and a monthly subscription for Post-it notes.

"I take it from the sour look on your face you were not a fan." Miranda tapped his knee.

Knox looked down. Her fingers had already disappeared but part of him still felt her touch. "I prefer fantasy. Wizards, dragons, magic."

"Wizards and dragons?"

Her smile made his heart leap. "Yep. The more fire magic the wizard uses, the better!" He made a few motions with his hands and she giggled.

He finished his coffee, hating the sign that their outing was nearing an end. "I can't listen while running, though. For that, I have to have a beat. I tried listening to podcasts that I enjoy since there never seems to be enough time for all the ones I love, but I couldn't make myself actually run at a good clip."

"Why do you have to run at a good clip?" Miranda raised her eyebrow as she used her straw to pull the last of the whipped topping from the bottom of the cup.

"I—" Knox sat there, trying to figure out the answer. "I—"

"You already said that." Miranda laid her hand on his knee and this time she didn't pull it away. "Just something to think about."

"Want to get dinner Sunday?" The question popped out, and he placed his hand over hers on his knee. He had no idea what this was, but he wanted to spend it with Miranda.

She looked at his hand then back at him. Her dark eyes holding his. "Like a date?"

"Yeah. Exactly like a date." He watched the wheels turn in her eyes. Saw the heat dance across her cheeks.

Say yes.

"All right."

The urge to pump his fist was nearly overwhelming but he kept it in check. "I'm looking forward to it."

CHAPTER SEVEN

"MIRANDA!"

Lacey, one of the floor nurses, walked up with a look she knew spelled dread.

"Jill has an infection in the wound on her left side."

Miranda took the tablet from Lacey and glared at the admitting notes under Jill's name. The woman had been discharged to a rehab facility only two days ago. Miranda was hoping not to see Jill again.

That was the weird part of being a trauma surgeon no one talked about. You saw people at their lowest. Saw them crushed and got to witness miraculous recoveries. And you hoped, fervently, that when they walked, or were wheeled from your care, that you didn't see them again.

"How is she mentally doing?" Infection in abdominal wounds was not uncommon but any setback was unwelcome, particularly because she knew how much Jill wanted to get home.

Lacey looked to the closed door of Jill's room. "Not well. I mean, no one likes coming back, but she seems down on herself."

"All right." Miranda made a few more notes in the chart and then moved to the door, knocking before opening it slowly.

"Jill?"

"Dr. Paulson." She blew out a breath.

Miranda couldn't see her face in the dark room. "Would you like me to turn on a light?" There'd been no mention in Jill's file about a headache or sensitivity to light, but it happened. It was also a key indicator for depression.

"If you like." The unenthusiastic response barely made it to Miranda's ears, even in the small room.

All right. Address the infection, then address mental health—at least as much as she was able.

"Tell me about your pain."

"Didn't the rehab send along the notes?"

Bitterness after a major life-altering event was not uncommon but she'd hoped Jill might avoid it. "They did. But you are the one living in your body."

"And I am the one responsible for what it can and cannot do."

The tone made Miranda see red. "Who told you that?" Jill had had major abdominal surgery. She needed at least a week in the rehab facility to help her regain strength in her abdominal area. People didn't realize how much the core muscles did until you had to slice through them!

"No one." Jill pushed a tear off her cheek. "It's just something I know. I mean, as you said, I am the one living in the body. If I cannot make myself do it, then who else's fault could it be? If I fail…" She pushed herself up on the bed, glaring at her stomach.

"It's like it won't do what I say!" Jill gritted her teeth then burst into tears.

Miranda sat on the edge of the bed, waiting for Jill to collect herself. This was a difficult time but beating herself up wasn't going to make the healing go faster.

"Sorry." Jill swiped at her nose as Miranda offered her a tissue.

"You don't need to apologize. You've had a setback."

"Setback. Such a diplomatic word, Dr. Paulson." Jill bit her lip. "Man, I really am being a bitch, and I don't even mean to. I am just so frustrated."

"Understandable. You aren't even close to my most difficult patient, but we do need to get the infection under control. Based on the notes I saw in your chart it looks like you might have overdone it at rehab."

"That place stinks. I don't mean like I don't want to be there, I mean it has a barely covered antiseptic odor that is not working at covering the scent of decay." She squeezed her eyes shut, balling up her fists. "I just want to go home."

Miranda understood. And she even understood the comment on the smell. Just like hospitals, rehabs had a unique aroma that made some patients uncomfortable.

Taking a deep breath, Miranda tried to keep

her words kind but forceful. "You have an infection. It's easier for your body to get infections if you are tired, or pushing yourself harder than you should. I know you want to go home, I do, but your body is not failing you. You are not failing. You are healing."

"Okay." Jill's lip wobbled a little more. "I don't suppose there are any paints in the cupboard you pulled the colored pencils and coloring books from?"

"There aren't but I will see if I can dig some up." Miranda was looking for things to add to the cabinet Knox had started. She'd seen a few people adding to it. Before long, they'd need another cabinet, or a closet.

"Thanks." Jill sounded more upbeat.

However, that could be so that Miranda wouldn't ask any more questions. She put in a psychology consult. If depression was at play that would slow Jill's recovery, too.

"If you need anything, let the nurses know."

"Just for my body to do what it needs." Jill smiled, but it didn't touch her eyes.

"Give it time." Miranda nodded before heading for the door.

Stepping out, she rammed into Knox.

His arms wrapped around her waist to keep her from falling over. "Careful." He raised his brows in a playful manner. "We have to stop meeting so abruptly."

"Do we?" Miranda chuckled as she stepped back. As much as she enjoyed his hands around her waist, they were at work. Tomorrow, though. Tomorrow they'd be on a date.

A date with Knox Peters. If someone had told her when they were interns they'd be going on a date she'd have laughed at them. And privately celebrated.

She wasn't the same woman she'd been, but the crush on Knox, that was unchanged.

"At least in the hospital." Knox lowered his voice. "Outside of it…"

He shrugged and she was sure there was a joke that wasn't work appropriate in his unstated words.

"How is Jill?"

"Blaming herself." Miranda let out the frustrations she hadn't wanted her patient to see. "She is blaming her body for failing, or more accurately blaming herself for her body failing."

"Let me know if you want me to do a secondary consult for psychology. Those guys are the definition of overbooked. Sometimes a secondary consult request speeds things along."

Miranda looked at the door. "Do you need to wait a few hours for that?" At her last hospital, the general rule was to wait two hours before doing the secondary consult for psychology. It wasn't the doctor's fault; the specialty was overburdened and not enough med students were finding their way in.

"Played this game before?"

"Who hasn't?" Miranda leaned against the wall and rubbed her back. "Even with the warnings that you will do so much more than just cut and heal patients, you never realize how much literal red tape there is just to get your patients the support they need."

"Back sore?"

She appreciated the change of subject. Complaining about administrative headaches wasn't going to fix anything—unfortunately. "Always. Isn't yours? We aren't exactly young guns anymore."

Age wasn't something that bothered her. Work in trauma surgery and you figured out really fast that getting old and creaky was a blessing so many didn't have.

"It's like my bones are screaming some days. Don't tell ortho!"

She let out a giggle that died as soon as both their pagers went off.

"Damn it." Knox looked at his pager. "Three GSW inbound."

She took off as soon as he did. Gunshot wounds... three of them.

It was going to be a long night.

Knox hit the elevator at the same time as Miranda. Three hours after their shift was supposed to end. They'd lost all three gunshot victims. A fight over less than fifty dollars had cost three young men their lives. It was the roughest way to end a shift.

The door opened and Miranda and he stepped in without saying anything. What was there to say when three lives were cut so short? Still, he scooted a little closer to her, and she did the same to him. They weren't quite touching but it was nice not be alone in the horror.

The doors opened on the parking garage and Miranda pushed off the back wall. "I hate days like these."

Knox wrapped an arm around her shoulder, then shifted and pulled her into a hug.

"I'm sorry." She hiccuped as the sobs started.

"Why on earth are you apologizing?" Knox stroked her back, tears coating his own eyes. Today was rough. So very damn rough.

"For crying." Miranda let out another sob and then a hiccup. "For getting emotional at all. I used to be able to control it. Now… Now it's like a monster let loose that refuses to go back in its cage."

"Miranda." Knox pulled back a little, making sure she saw the emotion in his own eyes. "There is nothing wrong with getting emotional over losing patients. Our surgeries were perfect. The fates just weren't in our favor tonight."

"The fates." She let out another sob. "Really?"

"Sure." Knox wiped a tear from her cheek then pulled her back into his arms. "We can do everything right, and sometimes it simply won't be enough. And the amount that sucks is immeasurable. Particularly when it was so avoidable. If any of them had walked away, or pointed differently or gone to the movies tonight or something…"

Playing the what-if game was never a great idea but it was difficult in times like this to ignore the possibilities. A millimeter to the right in his patient might have made a difference. He wasn't sure the difference for Miranda's patient but it probably wasn't much. The third had never made it out of the ER bay.

"Want to come to my place for a bit? I plan to pop some popcorn, eat candy and watch pointless television for a while." The offer flew from his mouth but he didn't want to yank it back. Going home to an empty place after a day like today could be a lot.

"Popcorn…not beer?" Miranda pulled back, shifting the bag on her shoulder.

"I have beer in the fridge if you want one." As a rule he didn't drink after a rough day. Knox trusted himself, mostly. But he acknowledged the addictive traits his mother displayed were in him, too.

He just made sure they were trained on things like besting others at darts and academic achievement.

"Come on, Miranda. Today sucked. It's well past dinnertime, but I doubt either of us is really hungry. So come eat popcorn and some chocolate at my place."

He waited for her to say no. Waited for her to make an excuse. Instead, she nodded then waited while he punched his address into her phone's GPS.

The drive home felt like it took no time and all the time in the world as he kept checking his rearview mirror to see Miranda behind him. Part of him expected her to change her mind. Instead, she pulled into the parking space behind him on the street in front of his condo.

"Is Jackson going to mind us watching television?"

"As long as it's not so loud that it echoes into his condo, no." Knox opened the door to his place, a sense of home settling through him as he dropped his keys on the tiny table he kept for that purpose right by his door. This was his sanctuary. His place. After a life lived out of trash bags operating as suitcases, owning his own place would never get old.

"Somehow I thought you two would always be roomies. A bit silly considering it's been more than a decade." Miranda followed his lead, taking off her shoes. The bright pink socks with kittens on her feet were a bit of a shock.

"Well, we are close. He's next door in the one we used to rent together. I bought this place when it went up for sale. He bought the one we lived in when the owner finally gave in to his pestering. So now it's just neighbors."

Knox headed toward the kitchen as he heard Miranda chuckle.

"I love my sisters, but I am not sure us living next to each other would ever be a good idea." She leaned against the counter as he pulled the popcorn off the top of the fridge and stuck it in the microwave. "Though I enjoy when Kelly and Olive stop by. And we have brunch on the first Sunday of every month. And given the six littles I play aunt to, it seems like there is almost always at least one birthday party each month. Family time is one perk of failure."

"You aren't a failure." Knox squeezed her shoulder, the motion not overly satisfying. "I'm glad you came back, too. But right now you're in front of where I keep the candy." Knox grinned as he slid an arm behind her. Her scent made him pause; he'd expected her to shift, to move over. Something. Instead, her dark eyes met his and his body nearly melted into her.

The one scrap of willpower he had from the day kept him from asking to kiss her. It had been a day. A terrible day. She was here for company, not for kisses.

He pulled the bag of mini chocolates from the cabinet, his fingers skimming her hips as he shifted. "Do you mind if I dump the candy in the bowl with the popcorn or do you want it in a separate bowl?"

Miranda's eyes held his, a look he hoped wasn't

disappointment floating across them. "I am crashing your downtime. Whatever you like best."

"Not crashing—a guest." He pulled the popcorn from the microwave and felt his body start to relax. This was something he'd done since med school. Though now instead of reading tomes of information trying to keep up with the woman beside him, he watched game shows or reruns to television shows he'd seen so often he could quote them.

"This way!" He held up the bowl, marching toward the couch, before realizing that his small couch was only really designed for him to sit on. As a rule, Jackson was the host. The one who wanted people to visit his place.

Knox gave it all at the hospital, then kept to himself here.

"I…um…" He pulled at the back of his head as he looked at his couch.

"Don't host much?" Miranda grabbed the bowl from his hands and sat on the sofa. "Guess we are just going to be comfy, then."

I guess we are.

Knox slid beside her, enjoying the feel of her next to him. "This does make it easier to share the popcorn."

He grabbed the remote, trying to ignore the rush he felt as her body leaned close to his.

Focus on the television.

"So what does Miranda Paulson like to watch? Documentaries?"

She made a face. Her nose scrunching so tightly her eyes closed.

"Okay, no documentaries. How about game shows?"

Miranda shrugged. "I had to watch a lot of game shows growing up. They are fun, provided you're not going to have me try to beat the buzzer."

So nothing in her family was done just for fun.

"All right, so I will show you my favorite game show, provided you tell no one. Not even Jackson."

"Not even Jackson." Miranda's eyes widened and her mouth fell open. "I promise. I swear." She put her fingers over her heart. "I swear."

"You already did that."

"I know." She grabbed a piece of popcorn, her grin wider than he'd ever seen. "But a secret that Knox Peters hasn't shared with his brother and best friend. I swear I will take it to the grave."

Knox shook his head and pulled up the show. Three women stood on one side of the stage while a man stood on the other. Nine suitcases stood between them, each bigger than the last.

"What kind of show is this?" Miranda grabbed more popcorn, her fingers touching his.

The contact brought a sigh to his lips that Knox barely managed to catch. She was here, at his place, eating popcorn and about to watch Baggage...the worst train wreck of a game show he'd ever secretly loved.

"Dating game show...sort of. The idea is that

each piece of luggage has some piece of personal baggage in it. The person choosing the dates throws out the one they don't think they can deal with and the person with that baggage leaves. There are two sessions—one with a female picker and one with a male. Winners get a date paid for by the studio."

Miranda looked at the television as the first suitcases opened, revealing some very personal details. "These are the little pieces of baggage?"

"So they say." Knox chuckled and threw his arm around her shoulder. The motion had been so simple, felt so right, but that didn't stop his heartbeat from pulsing in his ears.

Miranda's gaze held his before she slid just a little closer. "This is ridiculous."

He wasn't sure if she was talking about the show or the feelings racing between them. "It is. But everyone has a guilty pleasure."

"I never liked that term." Miranda leaned her head against his shoulder, started to lift it, then let it stay. "If you like something, it can just be something you like. And I guess it is nice if your partner tells you up front they cheated on their ex-fiancé with the fiancé's twin brother. How is that the small baggage?"

Knox laughed and leaned his head against hers. "The things people admit to on this show will absolutely make you feel better about your life choices."

They sat on the couch letting three twenty-minute shows play out before the popcorn and chocolate were exhausted.

"Do you want me to get more?" He wasn't hungry, but Knox wasn't ready to say goodbye to whatever this evening had turned into.

"No." Miranda's voice was soft. She lifted her head off his shoulder.

Her gaze was like water to his parched soul. His eyes fell to her lips, the pink mounds calling to him. "Miranda." Her name fell unbidden from his mouth.

"Knox."

Time hung between them.

"I want to kiss you." His hand rose, his fingers caressing her cheek.

"Kiss me."

Miranda's body sang as Knox's lips connected with hers. The fantasies she'd let herself indulge in during their residencies were nothing compared to the feel of him holding her. He felt safe, and luscious and like the world was calling for them to never part. Fantastical feelings, but indulging for a few moments couldn't hurt.

Her plans for tonight had not included sitting on Knox's couch watching the weirdest "game show" she'd ever seen. But it was far better than sitting alone in her place reading.

His hands slipped down her back, and she let

out a soft moan. "Knox." She wanted to lose herself in him. Wanted to throw away all the reservations her brain had no trouble spewing constantly and beg him to take her upstairs.

"I should get going." Those were not the words she wanted to say, even if they were the "proper" ones.

Today was a lot. Finding comfort in the arms of another was a stereotype for a reason. She liked Knox. If she went to bed with him, she wanted it to be because they both wanted it, not because they were reminding themselves that they were alive.

"All right." Knox dropped another kiss on her cheek.

"All right." She smiled and leaned her head against his. "Thank you for tonight. It was perfection. And now I know you like trash game shows where people spill far too personal secrets."

Knox's chuckle carried through her soul. "Well, I know that under your very professional-looking orthopedic shoes you wear pink kitty-cat socks. So we both know something about the other. Though your socks are hardly blackmail material."

Miranda looked at her feet; the cute cats always made her smile. "I love cats. Their little noses and snuggles."

"What was your cat named?"

She shook her head, kissed his cheek then forced herself to stand. If she stayed beside him any longer, she'd kiss him again and they would end up in bed. Miranda's dating record wasn't long, but she knew what her body was craving.

"I've never had a cat." She wiggled her toes as she headed to the foyer where she'd taken off her shoes. "Lance wasn't a fan of animals and my parents—" She waved a hand. She'd begged her parents for a cat. Promised to take care of it and they'd told her that if she got a perfect score in math her freshman year that they'd consider it.

A perfect score.

She'd nearly done it, too. But she'd missed one question on the final. One question. Ninety-nine percent was not perfect. So no cat. They'd never again made such a promise—though she'd gotten a perfect math score every year after.

"You could get yourself one now." Knox's hand was on her back as he opened the door.

It was warm and the urge to lean into him pulled at her. She ached to close the door and rip the man's shirt over his head and worship his taut body.

"Hospital hours." She bit her lip. She'd looked several times, fallen in love over internet pictures, celebrated each time they were adopted and told herself they were better off with someone else.

"Cats are pretty self-sufficient. Heck, you could even get a dog. After all, doggy day care is a thing. Dr. Protes takes his lab every shift. The dog loves it, and he shows us the live videos of the dogs playing in the yard. Frequently! Don't ask him about Potato unless you want to hear *all* about him."

"Potato? How did he come up with that name?"

"Ask that question at your own risk, Miranda. A dog named Potato kinda make sense, but cats are typically more dignified." Knox kissed her cheek then leaned against the doorjamb.

The sexy pose made her mouth water. It was time to go but her feet refused to move off the front step.

"You like cats?" Somehow that didn't surprise her as much as she thought it would. Knox would look adorable with a big dog, but a cat curled in his lap? That brought tingles to her soul.

"Yeah. I had a senior cat adopt me right after med school. Lenny was an orange bundle of love that cried for food at all hours and thought sleeping on my face was the best place to be. I lost him about two years ago and the universal cat distribution system hasn't sent me another yet."

Miranda laughed. Her sister swore that was how she got her two cats. Sometimes the universe decided you needed a cat, and one would show up and make your place its home. Miranda didn't think that was how it worked, but who was she to judge?

"I need to go." She looked toward her car, then pressed her lips to his one more time. "Thanks again."

"Anytime, Miranda. See you Sunday. Wear comfy clothes!" He watched her walk to her car and was still standing in the doorway when she drove off.

CHAPTER EIGHT

"You hear the news?" Jackson took a sip of the giant water bottle that seemed to be connected to him when he wasn't in the OR.

"News or rumor?" Knox didn't bother to look up from the computer screen where he was entering surgical notes. He'd yet to meet a surgeon who enjoyed doing any of the paperwork that came with the job, but unlike others, he never put it off. No use letting this pile up!

"Is there a difference in the hospital?" His brother shook his head and held up a hand. "Hey, Miranda!"

Now Knox looked up. Miranda was rolling her shoulders, then pulling one arm across her body to stretch. Hours on your feet felt like a lot more once you were in your forties. "You okay?"

"Just tired. Looking forward to my day off tomorrow." She winked at him then turned her attention to Jackson. "Hi, Jackson."

"So I am not invisible." His brother laughed and gave Miranda a high five.

"No." Miranda shook her head. "What are you two discussing?"

"Hospital rumors." Knox hit the final button and closed out the notes of the surgery he'd done this morning. For the moment, his paperwork was finished.

"Rumors?" Miranda raised a brow.

"Or news." Jackson took another sip of water. "I heard it as news."

"Is there a difference in the hospital?"

Miranda's words were perfect. Knox raised his hand and she high-fived it, though he could see her confusion. It wasn't the connection he wanted, but they were at work. Kissing a colleague was frowned upon, though if they were alone, he'd at least brush his lips across her cheek.

"How are you two one mind?" Jackson rolled his eyes.

"It's obvious we haven't heard, Jackson." Miranda moved to the terminal and pulled up the notes section for the surgery she'd done in the OR next to him this morning.

"And equally obvious you are desperate to spill the beans. So what is the news?" Knox typed out a few more notes.

"We are getting a new head of surgery." Jackson held up the water bottle in a *ta-da!* moment then frowned as neither Miranda nor Knox responded.

Miranda's dark eyes met his and Knox shrugged.

"That is quite the rumor." Miranda looked at Jackson.

"Seriously, neither of you heard it?" His brother

frowned and looked at his watch. "I would have thought you'd both be in the running to take the position."

Knox's stomach clenched. He and Miranda were competitors. It was what their residency was based off. Always pushing the other to be better.

And she'd won, each time.

"I am sure if Dr. Lawton was leaving, he'd have told Knox." Miranda tapped out a few more things on the computer then turned.

Knox looked at her; there was no hint of competition in her eyes.

Her beeper went off at the same time his did. "ER consult. With ortho…"

Knox looked at the ceiling. "I swear the bone guys are all the same."

"Not always," Jackson murmured.

Knox looked at him, but he didn't say more. "Let's go."

"The ER is crowded," Miranda whispered, but he could hear the concern in it.

The crowd was doctors, nurses and staff members. That meant whatever was here was unique. Unique was interesting in medical journals. Not when you were the operating surgeon.

"Yo!" Dr. Patrick O'Sullivan raised his hand as he stepped beside Miranda. "You two know why we're consulting together?"

"No." Miranda looked at the orthopedic surgeon

then shifted her head to the people in the room. "But given the crowd…"

"Something fun."

"Patrick." Knox liked the doctor. He was fun and incredibly knowledgeable. He was also one hundred percent the definition of an ortho bro.

Orthopedic surgery was the only rotation he'd done where they told him he didn't need a stethoscope and meant it.

"I mean fun in the best way."

"I need the surgeons in room five." Alex, a nurse who'd been in the ER longer than anyone else, shooed people away. "If you stay, I will put you to work in the ER. We can use some help."

The exodus happened immediately.

"Never fails." Alex handed Miranda the tablet chart. "Twenty-one-year-old male, impaled rebar through his left thigh."

Impalement. Unusual, but not unheard of. Particularly around construction sites. That didn't explain the crowd.

"Oof." Miranda looked at the chart, her eyes widening before she looked up at Knox.

Alex handed Knox a chart. "Twenty-two-year-old male, impaled through his right thigh." She read the words out.

"Are they connected?" Patrick's words were soft, but his stance had shifted. This was the professional who had moved to Hope last year to get a bit of a break. Dr. O'Sullivan was one of the top surgeons in his field in Dallas, Texas.

"Yes." Alex let out a breath, her shoulders slumping a little.

"Wow." Knox hadn't meant to say the word but this was a first.

"They were daring each other to jump off the second floor of the construction site on Lincoln Street. Not sure the exact events but…the paramedics didn't want to separate them until you guys saw the X-rays and decided what to do."

"And why am I here?" Patrick raised a brow. He was right; if it was through the meat of the thigh it wasn't good but it didn't require ortho.

Alex pulled up an X-ray on the other tablet. "The femur of the twenty-one-year-old."

Knox covered his mouth. The man's femur was shattered. The femur was the hardest bone in the human body to break. Shattering it usually involved high-impact car accidents and the recovery took months.

"All right." Miranda looked to Knox. "You want to cut with Patrick or want me to?"

"I'll take the solo. Is anesthesiology already here?"

"Yep! Anesthesiology first, then you guys. I know Dr. Mitchel paged Jackson to get ready in the other surgical suite." Alex reached behind the nurses' station and handed the saw to Dr.

O'Sullivan. "They should be out enough for you to separate them."

"Ready?" Patrick looked to Miranda and then Knox.

Ready or not, it was time to cut.

Miranda rubbed the back of her leg with her other foot as she started to close the wound on Carter Telers's thigh. The young man had been out when they'd cut him and his best friend apart, but the dirt stains on his cheeks had tear tracks.

Patrick had put pins through the bone and the boy would be in traction for at least three weeks. Then rehab. With luck, he'd be back to himself by the end of the year, but it was likely he'd have a limp for the rest of his life.

"You applying for Lawton's job?"

Patrick's question caught Miranda off guard. She saw Jackson raise his head in her periphery. Clearly, the rumor was well and truly loose. If Hugh wasn't retiring, he needed to nip the rumors in the bud fast!

"I wasn't aware that a position was coming open." And she had no plans to apply. Once upon a time she'd wanted to be the head of surgery. Wanted it more than she'd wanted nearly anything else. In fact, she'd considered applying at her old hospital even when burnout was chasing at her heels, convinced that that would make everything better.

Maybe it would have.

She mentally pushed that thought away. It wouldn't have made it better. She wasn't cut out for that. She'd learned that the hard way. No need to repeat the mistakes of the past.

"Oh, it's the hospital's worst-kept secret." Patrick's face was bright and she could tell he was smiling behind his mask.

"I see." Miranda wasn't sure that was true. After all, Knox wasn't in the know, either, and the man seemed to live here.

"So, you my top competition?" Patrick tilted his head as he closed the wound on the other side of Carter's thigh.

"No." Miranda had been back at Hope for less than a month. She had no intention of putting in for a promotion anytime soon. Or anytime at all, really. One failure was enough.

"Really. That opens the field quite a bit, then."

"I suspect Knox will put in."

"He isn't competition, though." Patrick put the tools on the side tray. "Done."

"Of course he's competition." Knox didn't need her to defend him. He was a great surgeon. Knowledgeable on so many different trauma types. Cool under pressure. Dedicated to his patients. He'd be a good boss.

Patrick shrugged. "He's never left Hope."

That was true. She didn't risk looking at Jackson. No doubt he had his own thoughts. It wasn't technically a requirement that surgeons moved around. But typically, they transferred at least a few times. Dr. O'Sullivan had run a successful practice in Dallas and before that he'd been at a regional hospital in Ohio. He was also experienced as a level-one trauma center. Hope was good. It just didn't see as many patients.

Knox had nearly every additional certification a general surgeon could achieve. And he'd been loyal to Hope his entire career. But loyalty wasn't rewarded as much as it should be.

"I thought you were at Hope to take a step back?" That was what she'd heard, but people had all sorts of reasons for taking new positions.

Patrick's eyes met hers. "I am, but I'm not passing up an opportunity. Head of surgery here would be a nice stepping stone to something bigger."

That was true. Though her body curled at the words *stepping stone*. Hugh Lawton had been head of surgery for over twenty years. It wasn't likely they'd get that again.

"Closed." She set her own tools to the side.

"If you change your mind, you'll let me know?" Patrick tipped his head as he looked at the stats on the monitor.

"There isn't even a position to consider at the moment." How could no one pay attention to that piece of the scoop? "And Knox will give you good competition, should he choose to put in."

Maybe he wouldn't be the top candidate, but she didn't like that Patrick was just tossing him out because his breadth of experience outside Hope wasn't as large. Knox would make an excellent head of surgery.

Patrick's dark gaze held hers for a moment. "I didn't realize you two were so close."

There was nothing Miranda needed to say to that. "Carter needs to head to ICU. I'm going to check on his friend." She'd actually expected Knox to find them first. After all, their surgery had been the one with the shattered femur.

Nothing about the impaling was good, but on scales of disaster, Carter's case had looked worse.

Knox was sitting in the staff lounge; his head slung over the back of the couch. Eyes tightly shut.

She didn't say anything. There was no need. Whatever had happened, what he needed in this moment was not to be alone. Miranda sat close, letting her hand rest on his knee.

It was several minutes before Knox finally opened his eyes. "It took six units of blood to stabilize him."

Six was a lot. Anything over four was considered major blood loss, but she'd seen worse. "Six isn't—"

"The first time." Knox let out a breath. "It took six the first time to stabilize him."

"Did he make it?"

"I beat fate today." Knox looked at the clock and shook his head. "I think."

Touch and go was the nature of their game far

more often than they wanted to admit. A consult that looked like the easier case could turn into a nightmare. And it had for Knox.

"He is alive. Thanks to you, Dr. Peters."

"For now." Knox shifted, putting his arm around her shoulder. "And your case?"

"In traction." She leaned her head against his shoulder. "It was standard pins and closing."

"Standard." Knox let out a laugh that held no trace of humor. "They were jumping off a second-floor construction site. Nothing about this was standard. It was stupid and reckless and just plain stupid."

He'd said stupid twice but she wasn't going to point it out. "Eighteen is considered an adult. But as science now indicates, the human brain isn't finished developing until the mid-to late-twenties."

"And the prefrontal cortex is the last to finish. Why on earth does the part of the brain responsible for making good choices develop last? What kind of a design is that?"

Miranda didn't disagree. It was something that scientists and doctors knew well, but the average person was just beginning to understand. And it differed depending on life experiences.

"At their age you were putting yourself through college, but surely you did some dumb things." Miranda hadn't done much besides study but her youngest sister, the rebel of the family unit, had made some very questionable choices. Her youthful criminal record had been expunged but that didn't wipe the memory away. Luckily, Olive's indiscretions hadn't hurt her or anyone else.

"I didn't have the luxury of doing dumb things."

Such a heartbreaking statement. She understood, but not in the same way. Olive had basically been cast out by her parents. They'd given up on her, and demonstrated to Miranda and Kelly they had the capacity to do what they threatened.

However, she'd had a roof over her head. Her parents had largely quit talking to her, but she'd not been shipped off.

"You did your best." Miranda squeezed his hand.

"What if your best isn't good enough?" Knox rolled his head from side to side then slapped his knees. "All right, I want some coffee to push the gloom away. Any chance I can convince you to get something sugary?"

Miranda saw the compartmentalization. Every medical professional had to develop it. It was the right choice, but she still worried for him. "I'm getting extra whipped cream."

She'd found out what it meant to learn your best wasn't good enough. It had crushed her, and rebuilding her life was still in phase one. What would happen if Knox couldn't compartmentalize anymore?

CHAPTER NINE

A DATE WITH Miranda Paulson. He was headed on a date with Miranda Paulson!

Knox practically danced up the stoop to her condo. The woman lived less than three blocks from him and Jackson. Frequenting the same coffee shop was going to happen on the regular. And he was looking forward to it.

The door opened before he even raised his hand.

"Can you give me one second?" Miranda pointed to the phone in her hand. "Knox, so good to see you. Come on in. Yes, Olive. I was talking to you about giving me a second. And yes, Knox is here. I told you I had a date. Yes, a date with Knox. Yes, that Knox."

Rosiness coated her cheeks as she motioned for him to step in and mouthed an apology.

That Knox.

So she'd talked about him. The warmth in his belly bloomed, and Knox couldn't keep the smile off his face.

Her condo living room looked like a library. There were six bookshelves overcrowded with books. He stepped to the first shelf and saw the standard medical journals and textbooks. He preferred to read these on a tablet. That let him make notes in margins and pull up the images to huge sizes. Jackson thought it was hilarious and enjoyed commenting on "old" eyes needing larger fonts.

Getting older was something many of their friends in the youth home hadn't gotten to do, so Knox wasn't overly concerned by the need to make a picture bigger or the few extra lines around his eyes.

The other bookshelves. All five of them were stacked with self-help books and journals. Titles like *Be Your Best, Organize Everything to Ease your Life, How to go from Zero to Hero.*

The only thing missing was one called *How to Exhaust Yourself!*

He had a room dedicated to an old television show he'd watched growing up. Jackson got him a memento or a toy associated with it for every holiday and birthday. A treat for something he loved but couldn't have as a kid.

These shelves… It was more than just listening to podcasts and audiobooks while running. More than not watching television. At least part of Miranda believed she needed these.

Believed she wasn't already the best version of herself.

"Sorry, Olive's youngest has a fever and rash. It's fifth disease, but she's worried." Miranda shook her head as she grabbed her bag from her purse. "The pediatrician is booked with flu patients, and Olive was worried so it's doctor sister to the rescue."

"I'm sure she appreciated that." Knox dropped a kiss to her cheek, enjoying the soft scent of lemon and sugar that seemed to cling to her. If he had any siblings, he wasn't aware of them. He never got to play the role of family doctor.

"It's weird to see Olive with kids. She is so overprotective. The rebel sister turned nurturing mother who will go feral if anyone tries anything on her kids."

She let out a sigh that Knox knew well. The sigh that said *If I'd had that...*

It was weird, heartbreaking and sometimes cathartic to realize you'd be a different person—a happier person—if you'd been raised in a happy home.

Wrapping an arm around her shoulder, he kissed the top of her head. "Ready for our date?"

"Yes." Miranda kissed his cheek.

For a first date they were already so comfortable. Thank goodness because after their first kiss, he needed her. Not in a sensual way—though that was there, too. Just in the way she fit with him. It was a weird feeling, one he'd never experienced before.

"So, now can you tell me where we are headed?"

"Nope. Still a surprise." He held her car door open with a flourish. He'd planned this from the moment she'd said yes. Well, not actually. The first plan he'd had was a fancy and expensive dinner date. Something he still wanted to take her on. But today, today was about the Miranda he learned about the night she came to his place.

The drive to the location took about ten minutes. If she liked this, perhaps she'd finally let one of her dreams come true.

"A cat café?" Her dark gaze glimmered as she shifted her head from him to the café over and over.

Knox had found the place as soon as she left his house the other night. He'd heard a few of the nurses mention it but hadn't put much thought into coming. Another cat wouldn't be his Lenny but he could love on a rescue for a bit.

"The cats aren't actually in the café part." Something he'd learned from the nurses when he'd questioned how they maintained their food licensing with animals roaming around. He could still recall Petra's look of absolute shock that he couldn't figure that out on his own.

"I assume they are in their own room."

"Yep, with a window so we can watch them play and probably sleep." He squeezed her hand, not surprised that she hadn't needed the explanation. "You have to have an appointment to meet the cats."

"Oh." Miranda nodded. "Of course. You can't just let everyone wander in."

"Our appointment is—" Knox looked at his watch "—in five minutes…then we can get coffee after."

"Knox!" Miranda laughed and nearly bounced out of the car. "You brought me to meet cats for our first date."

He exited the car, enjoying her brilliant smile. "It's different."

"It's perfect!" She pulled the door open and Knox wondered if she might dance her way inside.

He checked them in, and they filled out paperwork before following a young white woman with purple hair through the side door. She gave them instructions, which basically came down to let the cats choose what to do, and told them they had thirty minutes.

They stepped into the room and Miranda let out a soft sigh. "They are all so pretty."

She was definitely a cat mom. Because there were several of the rescues that were not what the average person would call pretty. More than one had at least one ear with a piece taken out, and two had chopped tails. Indicators that while this was a cat café, it was also a rescue.

Miranda sat cross-legged in the room and an orange tabby that looked so much like Lenny climbed into her lap.

His heart pounded in his chest as he watched her rub the cat's head. The rumbling in the cat's chest while the beauty he was with cradled the feline made Knox want to freeze this moment forever.

"His name is Inferno." Miranda made a face as Knox slid beside her.

"Not a fan of the name." Knox raised a brow. It wasn't what he'd name such a sweetheart, but rescue names were often temporary things that they hoped caught enough attention to get the cats adopted.

"This is a Cinnamon if I ever saw one." Miranda rubbed her head against the cat's. "Though he doesn't smell like cinnamon."

Knox laughed. "She just called you stinky, Inferno!"

Miranda opened her mouth, then playfully glared at him. "Don't listen, Inferno. You are very handsome."

The cat meowed, yawned then sashayed away.

"You hurt his feelings." Miranda tsked.

"I believe you called him stinky." Knox pet the head of a tiny gray cat nudging his leg.

"Careful, Miranda, thinking of names for a cat, even a stinky one, is a good way to adopt a cat." Knox personally thought Miranda should think of adopting. The woman had wanted a cat since she was a child. At forty years old she should grant herself that dream.

The gray cat climbed into his lap and started purring. It was an addicting sound.

"These little guys deserve better than my place." Miranda dropped a kiss on Inferno's head.

"Miranda—" How could she not think that a cat would love roaming her place?

"I just mean that I am gone a lot." She laughed

as a black-and-white cat named Fred dropped a play mouse in her lap, clearly waiting for her to throw it. She did, and shook her head as the cat brought it back and dropped it in the same place. "I thought dogs were the ones that played fetch."

The point of this date wasn't to get her to adopt a cat. Though he'd stop at the pet store on the way home if she decided to fill out an application. But he wished she understood that what an animal needed was love. Miranda had that in abundance.

"What is that little one's name?" She looked over at the gray one. "Smokey?"

Knox knew from their website that the café only had adult cats; that meant the little one in his lap was probably the runt of her litter. But she was sweet.

Looking at the name tag, Knox let out a laugh. "Nope. This is Bitsy."

The gray cat let out a yawn.

"I think she likes it." Knox rubbed her chin, grinning as the cat lifted her head, directing him exactly where she wanted to be petted.

When the woman came to let them know their time was up, it felt like only seconds had passed.

"It was so nice to meet you guys." Miranda threw the mouse one more time for Fred and then waved to the room. "I hope you all find the best homes ever."

Her eyes were bright and she was beaming as

they walked out of the room. "That was so fun! Maybe we should come back next week."

He'd bring her back anytime.

Knox wrapped his arm around her waist as they walked to the coffee counter. "You want the biggest frap with whip?"

She lifted onto her toes, capturing his lips. When she pulled back, she grinned. "You know me so well, it seems. Yes. I want the whipped topping."

Compared to most, Miranda didn't have a lot of experience with first dates. Her and Lance's first date had felt more like a job application—red flag number one of thousands. And the few others she'd had, if there'd been a spark, it was buried so deep no one was going to bother even looking for it. But tonight, tonight felt like it was the kind of date movies said everyone would experience.

The cat café, the dinner after, walking around the park and talking until the streetlights came on. Knox had thought of everything.

"Thank you for tonight." Miranda slid the key into the lock of her door. They'd been together for almost six hours, and she still wasn't ready to say goodbye.

"Thank you." Knox leaned against her doorjamb. His trim body so relaxed and delicious-looking.

"Do you want to come in? I can make some decaf coffee."

Or we can just go right up to my bedroom?

Her face was hot even though she hadn't let that last thought out.

"I'd love some coffee." His eyes sparkled with what she hoped was desire.

Opening the door, she slipped her shoes off, aware that he glanced at her feet. "Yes, I have a whole drawer of cat socks." These were blue with gray cats that looked very similar to the tiny cat that had sat on Knox's lap for most of their time in the café room.

"Nothing wrong with that. It makes me happy to think I chose right for the date."

She wrapped her arms around his neck, pulling him so close. "You chose right." She brushed her lips against his. The soft, playful kiss she'd meant to give him morphing into something more immediately.

Knox's hands pulled her closer, her hips brushing against his. She wanted him, now.

Pulling back just a little, she looked to her kitchen. "Do you really want coffee?"

"If you do." Knox's fingers danced along her back, tiny sparks of need lighting with each touch.

If this was how her body reacted to his touch over her clothes, how would it react to him touching bare skin? Only one way to find out.

"I want you."

The smile spreading across his face was the sexiest thing she'd ever seen. "The feeling is very mutual." She pulled away, grabbed his hand and led him to her bedroom. Her condo was nice, spacious, but in this moment she wished there were fewer steps from her foyer to the bedroom.

She opened her bedroom door and immediately pulled her shirt off. "I want to feel you touch me." The words were fire but the blink of fear spread through her. Lance had not enjoyed her taking any form of control in the bedroom.

Knox tilted his head and let out a breath. He raised a hand, letting his finger trace along her belly. "You are gorgeous."

"Says the handsome surgeon who looks like he belongs on a movie set instead of a surgical suite." Miranda lifted his shirt over his head, her eyes catching on the tattoos covering his chest and arms. There was a caduceus, a stethoscope and a bird breaking out of a cage.

"Damn, Knox. I didn't think it was possible for you to be hotter."

"You're going to make me blush." Knox bent his head, his lips trailing along her neck.

His hands found her bra strap, pulling it off. "Seriously, Miranda. You are breathtaking."

Knox's thumb circled her nipple, his eyes watching her as she melted in his caress.

The urge to strip him naked, join their bodies and ride the wave of fire pulsating through her warred with the need to draw this out as long as possible.

Knox's tongue flicked the raised bud of her nipple. Her hands ran along his back, where more tattoos were blazed across his body. She wanted to explore him but her mind couldn't focus with the masterful strokes of his tongue.

His fingers undid the button of her pants, slid them over her hips, then he slipped to his knees. He pulled her panties off and licked her.

Miranda let out a soft cry. His tongue found exactly where she wanted him. His hands gripped her butt, holding her in place for him to worship her.

Letting her hands run through his hair, Miranda lost herself in the sensations Knox was driving through her. Heat, desire, need, everything poured through her as he drove her closer and closer to the edge.

"Knox." His name on her lips as she crested felt like a cry to the heavens.

His arms were around her as he lifted her, carrying her to the bed. "Miranda." His lips brushed hers as he unbuttoned his jeans. "Sweetie, tell me you have a condom. I need you. Badly."

She grabbed the condom from the top drawer of her nightstand. She ripped the wrapper open and slid the rubber down his magnificent length. When she got to the end of his shaft, Knox let out a guttural noise.

Knox sat on the bed, pulling her onto his lap. She wrapped her legs around him as her mouth worshipped his. They moved as one, as though they'd done this thousands of times. Their bodies seemingly knowing exactly what the other needed, what the other wanted.

His fingers dug into her hips as she rode him to completion, her name echoing around them as Knox found his own orgasm.

CHAPTER TEN

KNOX KISSED MIRANDA'S BACK, letting his hands trace her body. Waking next to her felt too close to a dream. The date he'd planned yesterday had gone on for hours longer than he'd planned. Yet, it hadn't been long enough. Even now, as he was lying in her bed, he wanted more time.

"I could get used to waking up in your arms." Miranda rolled over, her breasts pressing against his chest.

They'd spent all night worshipping each other. He shouldn't be able to get hard again, but his body had no desire to listen to the biology notes his brain had learned through med school.

"I would never guess you had so many tattoos." Miranda's hand traced over the caduceus on his left biceps. He'd gotten that one the day after he'd graduated from med school.

"Body art is personal, or at least mine is. Still, people make judgments about it. I spent my entire childhood judged as lesser. The stereotypes of the bad guy having the tats have shifted with the younger generations, but they don't sit on hospital boards. Yet."

Her fingers ran along his hip. Her lips caressing his chin. "I understand the medical stuff, it's you. Why the bird in the broken cage?"

How did discussing personal topics feel so right even when they were lying naked in bed after their first date?

"As a kid in the system I felt like everything was a cage. Making mistakes was one step closer to delinquency, and everyone seemed to expect that we'd end up in the prison system. I did slightly better as a white kid. Jackson heard from more than one foster parent that he was just a choice away from parole."

"That's awful."

He could tell from the look in her eyes that she wasn't surprised, either. It was an unfortunate truth that humans were biased creatures. Othering made people feel safer, and the consequences were lifelong.

"It is. I got this the day I turned eighteen. And then I had it redone after college when I had the money to pay a proper artist."

"It's beautiful." Miranda's lips traced the edges of it.

"You're beautiful."

She made a noncommittal sound as she started to trail her lips down his body. Her fingers seemed to have memorized every little spot that made him ache even more for her. And she found them with deliberate speed.

When her mouth covered him, Knox couldn't help arching. His body seemed to react on its own around her. She took advantage and gripped his backside just like he had done to her last night. "Miranda."

His hands wrapped through her dark curly hair. His mind was lost to all thoughts but pleasure.

"Sweetheart, don't make me beg."

"What if I want you to beg?" Miranda's dark gaze held his, her hand stroking his balls as she ran kisses up his shaft.

She was going to be the death of him—but what a way to go.

"Please, Miranda. I need you baby. Now."

Her eyes glittered as she sheathed him and climbed on him. He let his hands roam her taut body as she kissed him. Her movements were slow, they'd spent so much time joined, but the need, the need wasn't diminished at all.

"You didn't come home last night." Jackson raised a brow as Knox stepped onto his stoop.

"I wasn't aware you were tracking my comings and goings." Knox winked as he opened the door. "Everything all right?"

"I got this for Miranda's closet." Jackson held up two bags of goodies.

"Whoa." Knox grabbed the bags. "That was nice of you."

"Wasn't me. I told Patty about it and the next thing I know…" Jackson shrugged as he looked at the bags at his feet.

Patty was an ancient white woman at the free

clinic Jackson volunteered at. The woman looked the same today as she did when Knox and Jackson had visited the free clinic as patients. The woman was a walking contradiction to medical science. She'd smoked at least a pack of cigarettes a day since she was sixteen and drank whiskey every night. She said if it hadn't killed her by eighty-eight, she wasn't giving it up now. She ran the "arts" program on her own shoestring budget for the local kids in her neighborhood.

Mostly it was crochet and cross-stitch because that was what she could do, but the kids in the neighborhood had all learned. Jackson still crocheted occasionally, and Knox swore that the cross-stitch lessons had prepped him for surgical sutures.

Knox looked in the bag. Crochet needles and yarn filled one and the other had cross-stitching materials. "That was kind of her."

"She knows." Jackson winked and Knox laughed.

Patty did not suffer from a lack of self-confidence.

"So, did Miranda get a cat?" Jackson sat on the tiny couch.

"No." Knox tilted his head, looking at his brother. "Out with it."

"What?" Jackson raised his brows, but he rolled his shoulders, clearly getting ready to deliver bad news.

"Word in the surgical unit is that Miranda came back for Dr. Lawton's job. That she knew he'd be retiring in a few months, and this is her next stepping stone."

"Miranda came home…" Knox cleared his throat. Her reasons weren't his to share. And weren't a cover for a next career ladder climb. "That isn't why she came home."

"Besides, has Hugh actually said he's retiring?" Why did everyone forget that? Hugh would tell Knox. He would.

"No. But you know how the rumor mill is."

"Wrong. At least fifty percent of the time." Knox understood office gossip. It was even more pronounced in the hospital. Long shifts in high-stress situations resulted in people talking to pass the time or to ignore the pressure to scream, or cry, after a tragedy.

"But when they are right…" Jackson let out a breath. "There's more."

"Of course there is." Knox shook his head. "There is always more. But it's gossip."

"People say they don't think you'll be competitive for the job." His brother's words were rushed. Jackson held up his hands. "I didn't say it. But it's being said. I want you to know in case you hear it."

"If I want it, I can make it mine." Knox didn't doubt that. He'd been at Hope longer than anyone else. He knew the inner workings better than the entire board and most of the administrative staff. Hell, he was the one people asked to shadow most often. The fact that people would think he wasn't qualified, that they'd rule him out before the competition even started, stole a little of the past twenty-four hours of joy, but he wouldn't give it any more.

That wasn't fair, but he wasn't going to engage in rumors.

"I appreciate the heads-up, Jackson."

"Not sure I believe that." Jackson sighed as he stood. "See you at the hospital."

"Good morning, sweetheart." Knox handed her a coffee. "No whipped topping since it's the start of the day but if I guessed wrong…"

"You didn't." Miranda dropped a kiss on his cheek as they stepped into the elevator. "Careful, Knox. I might get used to this."

Her mouth was hanging open. She knew her mouth was hanging open. She'd had a great time on their date and in the hours past it. But it was one date. Her ex-husband hadn't bothered to do anything that didn't progress one of their careers… usually his. But she'd clung to scraps of kind words and tiny gestures.

The small amount of affection she'd craved after a lifetime of trying to earn it in her family had made her accept less than she was owed. At least according to her therapist. Miranda had agreed with the assessment and sworn she wouldn't fall into the trap again.

And she could. It would be so easy to get used to this. To him. To silly game shows and cat café visits and maybe even a cat. Jumping from one date and hot sex to getting a cat together. Talk about leaps.

She'd spent her life trying to be better. To get good enough. Nothing was ever enough. It was easier to stay on her own than want more and never reach it.

"Miranda, what thoughts are rattling around your brain?"

"Nothing. Well, nothing important. Just chastising myself for saying out loud that I could get used to this. I wasn't trying to put pressure on you."

That was the line her ex had used so many times. The second he felt like she was asking him for something he made her feel like she was weak for asking.

"Would that be so bad? If you got used to it?" Knox raised a brow, then pressed his lips to hers for just a moment. It was a soft kiss, a reassuring one.

Hesitation stole through her. She wanted to say no. Wanted to say it wouldn't be a big deal if she got used to it. But no one took care of Miranda. She handled herself. She'd needed to handle herself.

She was rebuilding her life. It wasn't rubble anymore, but she didn't quite feel steady yet.

"Miranda, I had the best time the other night. I want more of that. If you don't…"

"I do. I do want more. That terrifies me." Had he snuck truth syrup into her coffee this morning? Those were not words she planned to say in the quiet of her own head, let alone out loud to the man who'd explored every inch of her body this weekend.

"Ah." Knox let out a breath, reaching for her hand. "It doesn't terrify me. Not sure if that helps."

"It does." She squeezed his hand, happy for the connection before taking a sip of the mocha he'd gotten her. A little of the worry leaking away.

She'd never had passion. Part of her had worried that deep love could combust. So she'd dated men, even married one, who didn't make her want to lose herself. Logic kept you safe, if mildly unfulfilled.

"It's just a coffee, Miranda. It's not like I'm trying to plan our future children's names. Just getting your coffee." Knox hit her hip.

I'm not having children.

Four little words that she felt very strongly but the elevator opened before she could say them.

Which was good since the hospital elevator was not the place for this conversation, but before their next date she needed to at least let Knox know. At forty, she was entering the final years of her fertil-

ity metrics but Knox could technically have children for many more years. If he wanted children,
then she wasn't the right person for him.

"Miranda, you're needed in surgical consult
now!" Jenny the duty nurse's eyes were frantic.

Miranda took a giant gulp of the coffee Knox
had gotten for her as she turned to pass it to him.
"Thanks."

He held it up and smiled. "Good luck."

"All right, Jenny, what is so urgent?"

"We have a patient refusing treatment." Jenny
blew out a breath.

Miranda understood the frustration, but it was
a patient's right to refuse any treatment. "That is
her right, Jenny."

"I know. But Dr. Reedy is older and a male and
he's trying to convince her, and I think she is right
to refuse. But…"

Jenny stopped right outside the consult room
door. "She's asked for a surgical consult several
times and Dr. Reedy keeps delaying it. She de-
serves to control her own body and choices."

Miranda nodded, then knocked on the door.
"Come in."

The older male voice was craggy and the tufts
of white hair on his head were well past the "thin-
ning stage."

"Good morning, I'm Dr. Paulson, general surgery."

"We do not need general surgery." Dr. Reedy

crossed his arms, his eyes darting to the nurse in the corner then behind Miranda, where she was sure Jenny was standing. So this was a medical standoff. Three women, a female patient and an elderly OB/GYN.

"What is general surgery?" A young white woman sat on the exam table, her thin legs hanging out of the blue hospital gown, her face pale.

"It means that I do all sorts of surgeries rather than specialized surgeries. What is your name?"

"Amber. And I want a hysterectomy not another round of hormone shots or birth control pills that make me feel suicidal." She glared at Dr. Reedy before wiping a tear from her eyes.

"A hysterectomy is major abdominal surgery." Miranda kept her tone level. This was not a request many people made, and those who did often felt quite strongly about it.

"And you are not even thirty. What if your husband wants a baby?"

Dr. Reedy's words were not overly surprising. It was shocking the number of professionals who asked what a woman's male partner wanted. Something that was only a deciding factor, if the patient wanted it to be.

"I do not have a husband."

"Future husband, then." Dr. Reedy looked at Miranda, clearly hoping to convince her to chime in.

"Amber, why do you want a hysterectomy?"

Amber pushed a strand of dark hair behind her

ear. She really did look too pale. "This is my third trip to the ER *this year* for blood loss during my period. I know that if I took birth control that it would lessen the flow."

"If it is giving you suicidal ideations, hormonal birth control isn't an option."

"Was it really that bad?" Dr. Reedy asked rather condescendingly.

"Yes." Amber's cry broke Miranda's heart.

Medical professionals had a lot of training, but they were not living in their patients' bodies. Only the patient could tell you what they were going through.

"There is the copper IUD." Dr. Reedy looked like he wanted to roll his eyes.

"Those can increase menstrual bleeding. What about an ablation? That procedure destroys the lining of the uterus and drastically reduces menstrual bleeding or even stops it completely."

"Then she still couldn't have children." Dr. Reedy looked at Miranda like she was out of her mind.

That was not technically true, though women who had the procedure were warned to avoid pregnancy due to complications should an egg attempt to implant on the thinned wall of their uterus.

"Do you want children?" Miranda looked at Amber. She'd never wanted them, and she'd known that from the time she was a teen. Amber was in her late twenties. Old enough to know what she wanted and for that choice to be respected.

"No."

"You might change your mind."

"Dr. Reedy." Miranda pinched the bridge of her nose as she took a deep breath. "It is not your concern if Amber doesn't want children. She is so pale, that I suspect she is anemic."

"Her hemoglobin is at eight. The last time she was here, it was eight point one, the time before that seven point six," the nurse in the corner stated, nodding to Amber.

They were united in their fight for their patient.

"So not just anemic but severely anemic. Have you ordered blood for her?"

"It's being typed now." Dr. Reedy pursed his lips then looked at Amber. "I think it best if I am no longer your physician."

"Wha—? Are you firing me as a patient?" Tears streamed down her face. "Because I don't want children?"

"I will notify the practice that you are discharged." Dr. Reedy shuffled past Miranda.

"Sorry." Amber let out a sob. "I'm just so tired. So tired."

"Some of that is anemia." Miranda made a few notes in the tablet chart Jenny passed her. She requested another OB/GYN consult, but she planned to talk to Knox.

"Can you do the ablation?"

Miranda wished there were a way to say yes. Wished she could offer Amber a fix now. She steeled herself to deliver the bad news.

"No. You will want an OB/GYN to do the procedure."

"Except every OB I go to says the same damn thing." Amber pitched her voice, "You're too young. What if you change your mind? What will your future husband think?"

She took a deep breath. "Dr. Reedy is not the first to tell me he won't help me."

Miranda grabbed the chair and slid next to Amber. "Amber." She kept her voice low, soft, controlled. "I know you haven't felt supported, but look around you. Two nurses made sure I was here. I'm going to find you someone who will look at your whole history and wants. It may take another few months and I know that hearing that is not helpful. But we will get this worked out."

A knock at the door made them each turn; the phlebotomist stuck her head in. "The blood typing is done. I'm here with the transfusion."

"I have a transfusion every time this happens. Not sure why we have to type my blood each time. I am A positive."

"Safety." Miranda and Jenny said at the same time.

"Get a little rest, and we'll check back in on you shortly." Miranda nodded to Jenny, who followed her out into the hall.

"Who do you know who will do the ablation? I'm not sure I know anyone who'd be willing at her age." Jenny made a disgusted noise.

Miranda wasn't sure. She'd been back in Phoenix less than a month. The contacts she had were mostly located on the East Coast. But Knox had been in the area his whole career. With luck, he could give her a starting point.

"Knox!" Miranda's voice carried down the hallway, but she didn't seem like she was in a race to the surgical suite. Hopefully, that meant the surgical consult had gone well.

"No cutting?"

"Not today. Or at least, not right now." She took a deep breath, squaring her shoulders.

"What are you preparing for?" Knox tilted his head as she adjusted her stance again.

"Do you know any OB/GYNs that will perform an ablation on a patient under thirty with no children and no spouse?" Miranda looked at the tablet chart in her hand. "Patient has had abnormal menstrual cycles since she was twelve. Routinely seen in our ER for blood transfusions."

"Dr. Elaine Matre." Elaine was whom he always recommended. "And if she isn't seeing patients, all the staff at her clinic are top-notch."

"The patient doesn't want children."

"You already said that. And that is good, since getting pregnant after an ablation is counter indicated." Knox reached for Miranda's hand, squeezing it gently before letting it go. "Why the surgical consult?"

Miranda let out a breath and then launched into a story that Knox wished he were surprised to hear. Dr. Reedy, and many others, had a tendency to play the what-if card when a woman asked for a procedure for sterilization. What if you change your mind? What if your future partner wants kids? What if...

"No one ever asked me what my wife would think when I got my vasectomy. And I wasn't even twenty-five." Knox shook his head as he pulled up some notes on his tablet.

"You had a vasectomy?" Miranda coughed as she looked around the hall, her cheeks darkening.

"You don't need to worry. It's something I am pretty open about." It was a choice he'd made and never regretted. He'd spent his life in the system. Knox loved the life he had now, but it did not include a calling for children. His life was his patients. That was enough for him.

Some men were squeamish about the procedure. Worried that it might "affect" their abilities. So he answered any and all questions. It was simply a medical procedure he'd elected to have performed.

"You joked in the elevator about naming our children." Miranda's eyes were wide.

He had said that. She was panicking over him getting her coffee. He'd gone to the furthest extreme he could think of—children. "It was a joke. If you want kids—"

"I do *not*." Miranda laughed then covered her mouth. "Maybe I shouldn't laugh at that."

"Don't see why not. Kids aren't for everyone. If people realized that—" Knox cleared his throat. His mother should never have had a child. She hadn't wanted him, and even when she was in her short bouts of sobriety, she'd made that quite clear.

"But it makes sense why you would feel so strongly for Dr. Reedy's patient."

"He just dismissed her." Miranda leaned against the wall, rubbing her back. "I hate that. But luckily you know everyone in the area."

"Been here long enough." Knox chuckled.

"Some might say too long." Dr. O'Sullivan hit Knox's shoulder as he chuckled. "Just kidding, Dr. Peters."

"Right." Knox shook his head. "What is it with ortho and their jokes?"

"The bone guys seem to be the only ones that really get them, too." Miranda's head turned, following the orthopedic surgeon until he was through the doors of the employee lounge.

"Ever think of moving?" Miranda's tone was low.

"Not since a very cute doctor beat me out of a coveted position after residency." Knox made sure that his voice was solid. "I've had offers, but nothing that really struck my fancy." It was weird how you could blink, and years could go by.

"Why?" He nudged her hip with his. "Trying to get rid of me?"

"Not at all." Miranda leaned forward and kissed his cheek. Then her hand returned to her lower back.

"Why don't you let me massage your back this evening?" Knox ached to touch her. To run his hands on her. A massage, a quiet night in. It sounded like bliss.

"I think I might just let you do that!"

CHAPTER ELEVEN

"YOUR FINGERS FEEL DELICIOUS!" If she could purr, Miranda knew Knox's massage would have drawn the sound out of her. His thumb dug into the exact right spot on her back, and tingles radiated down her legs.

"How are you so tight?" Knox put a little more of the massage oil on her back and continued his slow, circular movements.

"On my feet all day, stress of surgery, hitting forty. Take your pick." She said the words and let out a groan as he found another knot in her back.

"You are just a ball of stress, sweetie."

Knox moved his hands onto her butt and Miranda let out a sigh. The massage had been nice, and longer than any other a male partner had given her. Now the hanky-panky was starting.

"Why are you moving?" Knox lifted his hands. "Did that hurt?"

She looked over her shoulder, raising a brow. "You touched my butt."

"Yep. Your low back muscles connect to the piriformis muscle. We may not be bone bros but we know the muscular system. Lie still."

Miranda laid her head back on the table and sucked in a breath as Knox's fingers dug in. "Oh, my God."

"Not said in the way I like most." Knox kissed her cheek. "Take a deep breath. Let's get the knot out and your back will feel so much better."

His fingers pushed and pulled across her butt, finding knots she'd had no idea existed. But as his fingers released them, her low back seemed to align more, too.

"All right. Now the shoulders." Knox ran his hands up her back using his palms to apply pressure and she sank into the realm of pure pleasure again.

"Miranda." Knox kissed her nose. "Miranda, sweetie."

"I like being called sweetie. No one ever calls me a nickname." The words were heavy on her lips; her whole body felt like it was floating.

"Well, sweetie, I think it's time for bed." Knox lifted her off the table he'd borrowed from Jackson—who'd put himself through nursing school as a massage therapist. The brothers were full of surprises.

Miranda yawned; her eyes seemed incapable of staying open. "Knox—"

"Yes, sweetie."

She smiled against his shoulder.

"You shouldn't have still been here, but I'm glad you were." Miranda didn't think she'd said the words. Her thoughts were mush after his fingers tantalized her so much.

All she knew was she was glad he was here.

* * *

Miranda rolled over in Knox's bed. Her body was sore, but not in a bad way. Her muscles felt like they were relearning what it meant to be comfortable. Had she ever been comfortable?

Probably not. After all, if you were comfortable that meant you weren't working. Not working meant you were slacking.

When she'd finally slept in during her marriage, from fatigue and depression, her ex had told her that her new-found "laziness" was the reason she was struggling.

But mornings like this seemed designed to lie in bed at least for an hour or so before starting the day's activities. Particularly when there was a sexy man who made your body sing next to you. She was glad that he'd been here when she walked back through the door. He was like a grounding force. She rolled onto her side and stared at the man in the bed next to her. She was so glad Knox was here.

Dr. O'Sullivan was right, though. If Knox cared about advancing his career, staying at Hope was the wrong move.

Air seemed to rush through her ears as she lightly ran her thumb along the sleeping god's jawline. She was falling for him. Maybe the crush she'd had on him so long ago was more than she'd realized.

They'd always seemed to act almost as one.

Even as competitors. In a world where there wasn't a valedictorian and salutatorian, a number one and a runner-up, a winner and a loser, they were nearly perfectly matched.

She let her hand run down his thigh, enjoying the swell of his manhood. Miranda kissed his cheek, stroking his chest.

His hand moved to her hip, cupping her buttocks. "I don't think there is a better way to wake up." Knox turned, pulling her leg over his hip.

His fingers stroked her, finding her core, and Miranda let out a moan.

"I was trying to turn you on." Her lips trailed along his chin.

Knox grabbed her hand, placing it on his manhood. "Mission accomplished."

She cupped him, enjoying the intake in his breath.

His finger skimmed her nipple, and she arched against him. His erection pressed against her and she guided him toward her.

"I have condoms."

"You've had a vasectomy. I've had an ablation. I'm comfortable if you are." Miranda wanted him.

Knox didn't hesitate. He slid into her, cradling her as he gently rocked them. This wasn't a rush to completion. A drive for orgasm.

It felt deeper. More primal.

"Miranda." Knox's mouth captured hers, his

tongue dancing in rhythm with his fingers as they skimmed across her electrified skin.

She'd never felt anything like the sensations he was driving through her body. His shallow strokes drove her closer to the edge but weren't quite enough.

"Knox." His name came out as a plea. A desperate one.

"Sweetie." He lifted her leg a little farther up his hip. It still wasn't enough.

Miranda arched her back and hooked her leg around him, pulling him on top of her. Her body sang as he entered her fully.

"So demanding." Knox brushed his lips against hers but still didn't change his pace as he slowly drove into her. The slow strokes were pleasure and the most blissful torture imaginable.

She wrapped her legs around him. "Faster, Knox." Bliss was so close, so close but she couldn't quite reach it.

"I like you demanding, sweetie." Knox dipped his head, sucking one nipple, then the other. "But I want to enjoy this for as long as possible."

His tongue flicked the base of her neck, and electricity shot through her whole body. She arched with him as he cradled her through the orgasm. When it was over, he started building another.

"Knox!"

"Nope. No better way to start the day."

* * *

"Want to go for a run?" Miranda kissed his cheek as she grabbed a banana off his counter. "It won't take me long to run home and grab my stuff."

"A run?" Knox let his hand run along Miranda's excellent ass. She was wearing cotton panties and one of his T-shirts. There was no sexier outfit in the world. "I'm a little surprised you can think of that. My body feels like it's made of rubber. Maybe I need to spend more time pleasuring you."

Her dark eyes widened as she laid a hand on his chest. "My body also feels spent. And my muscles are so relaxed from the massage yesterday. I feel like I'm walking on air."

"So what do you say we spend the day snuggling on the couch?" Knox kissed the back of her neck as he mentally calculated ordering in food and spending the entire day with Miranda.

"But we relaxed the other night." Miranda turned in his arms, her eyes bright with a smile.

The sincerity in her voice sent a chill down his back. "The other night?" Was she talking about when they watched movies…almost a week ago? She couldn't be.

"Yeah. The 'game show.'" She used air quotes around the words *game show*. It would be adorable, if it wasn't so sad.

"That was almost a week ago and we lost multiple patients that night. You can just relax."

She blinked and opened her mouth, then closed it.

"You know that, right?" Knox reached for her hands. "You can just spend time reading a book *for fun.*" A designator he wouldn't have to make for most people. But even her reading habits were kind of work.

"When was the last time you just did nothing for the day but have fun with no purpose?" Knox squeezed her.

Her eyes shifted to the side; her teeth dug into her bottom lip. "I don't understand the question."

He was humbled by her honest answer. Even as it broke his heart. Miranda didn't know how to relax. The woman's body had been a ball of knots last night. As much as Knox enjoyed loosening her up, he hated that she was so tight.

"I know you don't, sweetie." He kissed the top of her head. "But today we are not going for a run. We are going to have fun. Lots of fun."

"Doing what?" Miranda's brows narrowed.

"Well, that depends." Knox playfully tapped her nose. "Do you know what you like doing?"

"I liked beating you at darts." Miranda raised her chin, the dare in her eyes clear as anything.

"Because you like playing darts?" Knox enjoyed darts. It was therapeutic, even though he'd started playing for all the wrong reasons. Though those reasons weren't his.

Miranda twisted her lips. So the answer to that question was no.

"All right." Knox playfully turned her, tapping

her butt. "Today is operation figure out what Miranda likes doing just for herself. Step one. I get dressed, then we run to your place, get you dressed for the day. Then...we try a pottery place."

"Pottery?" Miranda looked over her shoulder.

"Sure." It was fun and you got to create. That might make her feel like she was accomplishing something. It was a start at least.

"When you said pottery, I thought you meant making the pottery." Miranda looked at the paint your own pottery studio and laughed. "I was already planning how to get pottery clay out from under my fingernails."

Knox squeezed her hand as he opened the door. "If you want to try making a pot we can. But to get studio time you need more than an hour to schedule it."

"I'm surprised you even know of these places." Miranda's smile was big; hopefully, this was a good idea.

Knox shrugged. "I wanted to have a birthday party here when I was a kid. Well, not here. But in a place like this." He'd known enough not to beg his foster parents for it. The answer wouldn't have just been no. It would have been hell no.

"So as an adult you came here to treat yourself?" Miranda hit his hip with hers.

"Honestly—" Knox looked at the walls of ceramics waiting for their glazes to turn them into something beautiful "—I've never actually come in."

He'd driven past the location so many times. Never pulling in.

"Well…" Miranda wrapped her hand around his waist. "Then what are you picking?"

He wasn't surprised when she chose a cat figurine, but he just kept staring at the options. The plates, the banks, the figurines. It was all so much.

"We can always come back and do it again." Miranda kissed his cheek as she handed the cat figure to the woman.

She was right. Knox was an adult, with adult money. If he wanted to spend his free time at the art studio he could do that. He reached for the turtle piggy bank, then pulled his hand away. What would he do with such a thing?

"Get it." Miranda grabbed the turtle piggy bank, placing it in his hands. "It's clear you want it."

Knox moved it around his palms. "One of the kids in one of the foster homes I was in had something like this. We weren't allowed in his room— he was the biological son. That mattered a lot in some homes."

Knox ran his fingers over the turtle's face. "It's silly to even remember it. But he had a turtle bank. I wanted it and I must have been seven or eight. I got caught looking at it. He claimed I was trying to steal his money. That was when I learned it was a bank."

He pulled his head back. That wasn't a story he ever shared, and it just slipped out with Miranda.

Miranda's eyes flashed but there was no pity in them. Instead, she raised her chin. "If you do not get that and paint it, I will put my cat back, go home and listen to an audiobook on organizing."

"Quite the threat." Knox kissed her cheek as he led her toward one of the tables, the turtle bank hot in his hands. This might seem silly but there was no way he was letting her walk out without the cat and having some fun.

CHAPTER TWELVE

KNOX RANG THE BELL TO Miranda's condo and entered as soon as she said to come in. The past two weeks had flown by in a series of date nights in and stolen conversations at the hospital. And tonight he had a surprise for her.

"I have something for you," Knox called as he slid his shoes off by the door. His eyes immediately going to the romance novel on the side table next to her couch. The fantasy and sci-fi books he'd recommended were a bust, but one of the nurses had recommended a romance. Miranda had devoured it. And the three others in the series.

It had gotten out that she liked romances, and a stack of recommendations was appearing from so much of the hospital staff. Apparently losing yourself in happily-ever-afters was a pastime many enjoyed.

And there were options for everything. Though he'd barely kept a straight face when she waxed lyrically about an alien romance that she'd devoured in a day. Whatever made Miranda happy was great!

Miranda came around the corner and leaned against the doorway between the living room and her kitchen. "Dinner is on the table. Street tacos from Julio's."

"That sounds right domestic." Knox laughed as he moved in to kiss her.

She deepened the kiss. When she pulled back, Miranda playfully pushed at his shoulder. "No one will ever call me domestic and mean it."

There was a tone to her words, one that made him reach for her hands. "Does that bother you?"

"No." Miranda shook her head as she moved to pour some wine. "I should have made margaritas but I don't have tequila."

"It doesn't bother you?" Knox took the wineglass. He didn't care what she offered him. They were together; that was all that mattered.

"It bothers me that it is supposed to bother me. I've achieved a lot. I'm rebuilding after burnout and divorce. But at forty I'm not married, don't have or want kids. Breaking all the unspoken rules of society." She rolled her eyes. "What did you bring me?"

She held out her hands, her eyes sparkling as she looked at him.

Knox pulled the gray kitten she'd made on their date day out of the bag. The squeal coming from the beauty across from him was childlike, melodic and rattled the windows all at once.

Miranda took the kitten figurine and laughed. "I don't know why this makes me so happy."

"Just think what a real cat might do." Knox pulled the turtle bank out of the bag.

"Your bank." Miranda set the cat on the counter and reached for the turtle. "Did seeing it make you as happy as the cat made me?"

No. It had made him happier. He hadn't squealed. Hadn't danced in the little studio, but a piece of his heart seemed to stitch into place when he held it. A little piece of childhood that he could gift himself. Those were a lot of words and emotions and he wasn't sure how or if he ever wanted to voice them.

"It's something special."

Miranda's eyes caught his. For a moment he nearly shifted under her gaze. Nearly spilled how the turtle made him feel deep inside. But it was a turtle bank. Something so insignificant. It felt ridiculous to give it that much power.

"Maybe I should put the cat on the cat tree I bought?"

"Cat tree?" Knox knew he hadn't hidden the surprise on his face, but who bought a cat tree and then didn't get a cat?

"Bought it on a whim." Miranda's cheeks were pink and he suspected that she hadn't meant to share any of that.

It was past time she had a cat. So now he knew his next mission; get Miranda a cat.

"Taco time!" Her phone dinged and she made a face that wasn't hidden quickly enough.

"Do you need to take that?"

"No." Miranda stuck her tongue out. "Just another hospital rumor text. I guess Dr. Lawton is retiring."

"That rumor is just a rumor. I talked to Hugh." Knox followed Miranda into the kitchen, his mouth already starting to water in anticipation of street tacos.

Knox wanted to roll his eyes. This rumor really was getting out of hand. Hugh had blown it off. Said not to worry too much over rumors. "I swear, hospitals are hotbeds of gossip but this is getting out of hand."

"Knox." Miranda's voice was level as she held up her phone.

Know three people on the selection panel. I will give you a run for your money, Miranda.

Dr. O'Sullivan's text had two emojis at the end. Somehow Knox hadn't pegged the bone bro as an emoji guy.

"Selection committee. Hugh hasn't even announced his retirement." Knox pinched the bridge of his nose. "There must be some misunderstanding."

"I don't think so." Miranda pursed her lips as she passed him the plate of street tacos. "I think Hugh is retiring."

"He told me he wasn't." Knox had been at the hospital longer than anyone else. He'd stayed when everyone else left. Hugh would tell him. He would.

"Did he say he wasn't? Or did he say not to worry?"

Miranda's questions made his stomach sink. "Not to worry." Knox had taken that to mean Hugh wasn't retiring, but that wasn't technically what he'd said.

"I've been at Hope longer than anyone else. When others have used it as a career peg to other things, I've built a career there. He should have told me." The tacos on his plate looked great but his urge to devour them had evaporated.

Miranda's fingers wrapped around his wrist. "You're right. But it's possible his contract means he can't tell us until the selection committee is set."

Her words rang true. Hugh was a stickler for protocols. He followed every rule, while Knox followed the letter, but not always the spirit. Like when he'd let patients know they could switch physicians. Technically, something that was allowed and guaranteed under the patients' rights, but not really something the hospital advocated for.

It was one of the things the board loved Hugh for and reminded Knox of when he teetered close to the line. If they'd told Hugh not to tell anyone that would include Knox. No matter how much that hurt.

He took a bite of the taco, trying to force away the emotions pooling in his stomach. "And Dr. O'Sullivan plans to give us a run for our money, huh?"

"I have no plans to put in." Miranda took a sip of her wine. "Do you?"

"Of course." Knox didn't know what stunned him more. That she wasn't planning to throw her name in the ring or that she had to ask if he was?

Miranda would excel at the position. Losing to her wouldn't sting nearly as bad this time. Though he still thought he had the edge.

Knox had been at Hope longer than anyone. The surgical suite was practically his second home. Hell, there were days it felt like it was his primary residence.

"Does Dr. O'Sullivan mention who is on the selection board?" Knox wasn't surprised the orthopedic surgeon was interested. But he wouldn't stay at Hope. Not for more than a few years. Hope was one stop on his career ladder, not the pinnacle rung. Something Patrick had not kept quiet.

Which was fine. People got to move on. But the patients and staff deserved someone like Hugh. Someone devoted to the hospital. Someone staying.

They deserved Knox.

"No." Miranda kept her eyes trained on her plate.

He waited for a moment, hoping to push away the uncomfortable feeling that she was avoiding meeting his gaze.

"I'll have to ask Hugh." Knox waited but she only nodded without looking at him. His belly twisted. Maybe tacos hadn't been a good idea.

Her phone dinged again. She looked at it and grinned.

Knox didn't want to act like a jealous boyfriend. Particularly because they hadn't officially discussed any labels. That was the actual plan for tonight in his head—before Patrick O'Sullivan's texts arrived on Miranda's phone. Still, he wanted to know what had caused such a grin on her face.

"More information from Patrick?"

"No." Miranda held up a photo. A tiny gray kitten was curled on the front stoop of a house.

He hated the sigh of relief that echoed out of his mouth. Miranda's eyes met his, but she didn't ask any questions about his sudden exhale.

"Cute cat. Whose is it?"

"That is a good question." Miranda ran a finger over the image on her phone before setting it aside. "Kelly has posters up around the neighborhood, but we suspect that it is a feral cat's kitten. It can't be much more than three months old. Kelly will take it to the shelter if she can't find an owner. Her dog is *not* a fan."

So it could be Miranda's kitten. If she wanted it.

"You could adopt it."

Miranda didn't acknowledge that statement; instead, she put her elbows on the table and leaned her head on them. "Why did you sigh with relief when I showed you a cat? Were you jealous that Patrick was texting me?"

"I want to say no. That I don't care if he's texting you." Knox shrugged; may as well address this head-on.

"But you do?" Miranda bit her lip and the worries about Hugh's potential retirement disappeared.

Her eyes were bright. There was a tint of pink in her cheeks, a hopeful sparkle in her eyes. "Do you want me to be jealous?" Knox reached for her hand, enjoying her fingers wrapping through his.

"No but also yes." Miranda let out a giggle. "Such a ridiculous response for a woman many years past her teenage self. Since we're on the subject, though, I'm not seeing anyone else." She took a deep breath. "And I don't plan to while we are dating."

"I feel the exact same." Knox leaned across the table, his lips brushing hers. "So do we label it? Boyfriend and girlfriend?"

More pink spilled into her cheeks. "It's funny. Some days I feel too old for such a label, but I want it."

"Then you have it." Knox stood, walked around the table and pulled Miranda to her feet. "We can clean up the dishes later. Right now I want to take my girlfriend to bed."

"Miranda, can we talk?"

She knew what Hugh wanted to talk about. The surgical floor was buzzing with the news. Confirmation of what everyone already knew.

"Have you talked to Knox yet?" Miranda wanted him to hear this as close to first from Hugh as possible. He'd been on the floor longer than anyone other than the surgeon in front of her.

Knox hadn't moved around like most of the staff. He'd done his residency here. Then gotten a position and earned certificates that made him competitive as hell at other places. Yet, he'd stayed. So he deserved to hear it early.

"No." Hugh looked down at the floor. "We had a patient come in with gangrene on the foot. Diabetic. He's doing the wound debridement, hoping to save the foot."

It was not an uncommon injury in diabetics. Nerve damage related to the diabetes could cause the loss of feeling in the extremities. If an injury occurred it could easily get infected, but the patient might not feel the pain.

"Think it will work?" Miranda was delaying Hugh's announcement. She knew it. He knew it. But she watched the older surgeon step into the role of head of surgery. His shoulders a bit straighter as his eyes held a truth he wasn't ready to admit yet.

"Not sure."

Which meant no. Knox was trying and it might work. But the odds were stacked hard against him. Today was going to be a hard day for her boyfriend.

"I'm retiring, Miranda."

"So I heard." She tipped her head then raised a

hand and patted him on the shoulder. "We'll miss you. Do you have plans?"

She hoped so. Miranda had seen far too many people retire, not know what to do with themselves and return. Her father had signed retirement papers three times. And all three times he'd returned to another company doing similar work because staying home and relaxing wasn't an option. The only thing that stopped his work was the grave.

At least she knew where she'd inherited the inability to relax.

"My wife and I have three cruises scheduled. She loves them and I haven't been able to go with her much. It's time for me to party on the high seas." Hugh looked down the corridor, then leaned back on his feet.

"But it's not my plans I want to talk about."

Nope. She wasn't having the conversation she saw dancing in Hugh's eyes. "Hugh…"

He held up a hand and the resident in her that had hung on every word the man said shut her mouth. "You would be an excellent head surgeon. Hope would do well under your supervision."

It was a kind thing to say. Two years ago it was exactly what she'd wanted to be told. She'd spent her life achieving. Head of surgery was as high as she could go and still spend time cutting. Any further up and it would turn to admin work.

The absolute bane of a surgeon's existence.

Today, though, this version of Miranda wasn't

ready. She overthought getting a cat; she gave patients and their families hope when it wasn't warranted yet. She didn't function at the level she used to.

Was her work solid? Yes. Was she still good? Yes. Better than most, even? Probably. But the certainty she'd had in herself, the belief that she could fix anything, had poofed out of existence in her soul.

The running joke in med school was that surgeons had God complexes. She'd once heard a surgeon say, *"Only because we are godlike."*

She'd never believed she was godlike, but the complex was real for a reason. You had to be certain in your duel with the fates that you would win more than you lost. That you were the conqueror.

Besides, she was happy with the life she was building. Maybe career was coming second, but she had Knox and her sisters, and her nieces and nephews. The dreams looked different now, but that didn't make them bad.

"You'd be great at this, Miranda."

The tiny ball of flame in her soul that brightened every time she could achieve flickered. If she tried, really tried, Miranda probably could make this a reality. Her chest tightened and her palms itched. The urge to achieve burned next to the withering cold reminder that she'd burned out so brilliantly not that long ago.

That should be enough to force the urge away.

"Hugh!" Jackson's voice was bright behind her.

Thank goodness she wasn't alone anymore.

"I just heard the good news." Jackson offered his hand to Hugh, gripping it tightly as he slapped the surgeon on the back.

"I feel like this was the worst kept secret in Hope Hospital's history."

Jackson nodded. "It leaked weeks ago. It is the way with big news." He sighed. "Retirement, man. You better enjoy it."

"I plan to." Hugh beamed. "I'm trying to convince Miranda to put in for the job. They selected the recruitment team. Which, for reasons I don't understand because I refused to do any unnecessary admin stuff, was the reason I had to play it cool despite everyone asking."

"Don't worry about it." Jackson parroted the line they'd all heard Hugh say over the past few weeks.

"You'll help convince Miranda to look at the job opening? She has refused to say anything. Which is shocking! The resident I knew would have jumped up and down at this opportunity to compete."

"That resident would never have returned to Hope." Jackson winked at Miranda.

She smiled at Jackson, appreciating the look he gave her. Not giving advice or asking if she wanted to put in. A simple acknowledgment of the woman standing here now. Unfortunately, it was clear from the look Hugh was giving her that he was waiting on a response.

A simple *I'll think about it*. That was noncommittal and easy. Or she could be honest and admit that she didn't feel ready for it. That she didn't really want it.

That was the right answer. But her tongue refused to utter the words that she knew would have disappointed so many in her past.

"Dr. Paulson." The nurse walked up, a smile on his face. "There is a patient demanding to see you."

Typically, Miranda didn't give in to demands. She'd run into more than a few patients who felt that because she was a female surgeon they could bully her. But she'd do anything to get out of this conversation.

"Of course." She turned, following DeMarcus. "What are the demands?" She mentally calculated her patient list. No one currently on it was someone she'd have pegged as difficult. But surgery had a tendency to bring out the worst in people. Pain did that—whether it was physical or mental.

"Just to see you." DeMarcus grinned. The black man's face was brilliant. Not exactly the face one expected when they were being harried by a disgruntled patient.

"DeMarcus?"

"Dr. Paulson!" Jill's voice was strong as she waved from the nurses' station.

"A difficult patient?" Miranda raised an eyebrow.

"I said a patient was demanding to see you.

Never said they were difficult." The man winked as he slid behind the nurses' desk.

"Jill." The woman looked good. They'd discharged her after her return from rehab almost two weeks ago. She looked better than Miranda would have guessed for this stage in her recovery. Though it had been more than a month since her attack. Her body was healing, and the smile on her face made Miranda's day.

She held up a platter of Dorothy's Cookies. The iced shapes made her mouth water. The cookies were a staple in the area. They were made by one woman—ironically named Betty—in her small bakery. She swore the buttery treats were named after her mother, who loved sweets more than anyone.

Miranda had no idea if that was a marketing strategy or the truth. What she knew was these were the best cookies in the city.

"I wanted to thank the staff for saving my life." She set the cookies down, then picked one up and placed the cookie in Miranda's hand. The cellophane-wrapped stethoscope was beautiful, and it would taste even better. "And I wanted to make sure *you* got one."

There were tears in Jill's eyes. "I wouldn't be here without you."

"I was just in the right place at the right time." Knox and Jackson were at the bar. They'd have saved her life.

"Not just the night at the bar. The talks and the information to help me get home. My bags are packed." Jill bit her lip then straightened her shoulders. "The counselor you recommended gave me a list of places. My mom is letting me move back into my old room. It's temporary and I was so afraid it was failure but it's not. Just a new dream, a step in a new direction."

A step in a new direction.

It was a good phrase. One she should start using with her patients…and herself.

"I am glad to hear that, Jill." She opened the cookie and broke it in half, popping one piece into her mouth. Miranda closed her eyes automatically, the sweetness of the cookie blending along all her senses.

Opening her eyes, Miranda smiled. "And thank you for the cookies. They weren't expected but I know everyone will appreciate them."

"Thank you again, Dr. Paulson." Jill looked to DeMarcus. "Tell the staff sorry I was a grump sometimes."

"You were fine." DeMarcus grabbed a cookie from the tray and put it in the pocket of his scrubs.

"I think getting stabbed is a good excuse for being grumpy." Miranda raised her hand and smiled as Jill returned the handshake. "Good luck. Have a great life. You've earned it."

CHAPTER THIRTEEN

"So, I DID SOMETHING." Knox bit his lip and pulled an adoption form out of his backpack as they walked to the elevator bank. An approved adoption form.

Miranda eyed the paper in his hand but didn't reach for it. "Meaning?"

She wanted a cat. Needed a cat. The little gray figurine still sat on top of the cat tree. It was such a sad little reminder that her home was ready for a furry companion. She'd be the perfect cat mom, if she'd just let herself.

"You are approved to adopt from Old Farm Cat Sanctuary." Knox shook the paper, hoping she'd take it.

Instead, she crossed her arms.

"You got me a cat?"

"Nope." Knox had not taken that route. She needed to pick a cat or rather a cat needed to pick her. But more importantly, animals weren't presents. "Though I will pay the adoption fee if you go and find a buddy."

"Find a buddy." Miranda's dark eyes held the paper in his hands. "I like the sound of that."

"But?" Knox raised a brow. He could hear the word hovering on the end of her sentence.

"But the hospital, but my life, but…" Miranda

let out a heavy sigh that he was sure contained so many unnecessary worries.

Knox put the application back into his backpack and pulled her into his arms. "The world is always going to have buts, sweetie. It is the way of life." He ran his hand along her cheek before pressing his lips to her forehead.

There were a million reasons not to do things. Hell, he'd found excuse after excuse to not leave Hope Hospital. But that didn't mean you shouldn't jump at opportunities, either—like the head surgeon job for him and a cat for her!

"This is just an approved application. And I was honest about everything. Your hours, how long the cat might be alone, the job you have, everything. The rescue reached out in less than two days— which is a minor miracle for an all-volunteer organization. They think you would be a good cat mom." He kissed her forehead again, wishing they weren't at the hospital so he could truly kiss her. "Only you are stopping it."

Miranda squeezed him tightly. "Lance hated animals."

The words were soft. Ones he wasn't sure she'd meant to speak. "Lance isn't here."

If he was, I'd give him a piece of my mind.

"I wanted a cat when my depression was bad. I thought it might help with burnout. Or at least give me a cuddle buddy on the days when getting out of bed felt too hard."

It probably would have. And even if it didn't, she clearly loved cats. A loving spouse would want their partner happy.

"Lance told me that expecting another living creature to help me was selfish."

Knox had never worked so hard biting his tongue. "I think we should go see the cats. If nothing happens, nothing happens. You don't have to take a kitty home."

"But I can." Miranda's smile was brilliant as she held her hand out for the application. "I can take one."

"You have everything you need, and even some things you don't!" Knox squeezed her.

"I don't have food." Miranda stepped back.

The wheels were turning. She'd rebuilt so many areas of her life. The woman was amazing; she just needed someone to help with this last step. And now she was off and running with ideas of what the till-now fictional cat might need.

"The rescue will give you enough food for at least a week. You don't know what cat you are getting. Kittens, adults and seniors have different dietary needs."

"Right." Miranda nodded. "When are we going?"

Knox looked at his watch. Maybe he should have waited until closer to their scheduled appointment. But on the random chance that Miranda wasn't sure about this, he'd wanted to be able to give the rescue a heads-up that they were canceling the appointment. "We don't have to leave for another two hours. We can head to your place, get the litter box ready and fill the water bowl."

"And after that, we can make out a bit, so I don't watch the clock the whole time until it's time to leave." Miranda clapped, the crinkles in the corners of her eyes deepening as she danced up to him and kissed him.

"That sounds like an excellent way to fill the next few hours!"

Miranda held on to the edge of Knox's car seat to keep herself from bouncing up and down as they pulled into the small rescue location. She was a forty-year-old woman but in this moment, she felt five.

When Knox told her he wanted to talk as they were leaving, she'd expected him to ask about putting in for Hugh's job. It felt like over the past two days everyone in the hospital had asked if she was throwing her name into the ring. Everyone but Knox.

They'd not broached the subject once. In the old days, they'd have started competing for the job right away. They'd have quietly and not so quietly started mapping out plans. Miranda would have pushed herself to the bone to make sure she came out on top. Whether she wanted the job or not.

And she didn't want this job.

She was back at Hope, finding herself again. Stepping back. That was what she was doing, what she planned. It was a good choice—it didn't mean that she was letting failure get the best of her. Just that she was choosing her path.

And her path was at Hope. But not as the head surgeon. She rebuilt her life and for the first time ever, she was the only designer. Not her parents, not her ex-husband. Miranda was deciding.

She tapped her foot, grateful when Knox pulled the car to a stop. She wanted to see the cats. Hopefully, she'd even take one home. Knox had dusted off the soft carrier she'd picked up years ago. It had moved back to Arizona with her, even though she hadn't even visited a cat rescue.

"Ready?"

Knox's smile filled his face. He was so excited. What happened if this was a bust? Would he be disappointed?

"I'm not sure. I mean, I want to see the cats. Obviously." She blew out a breath trying to keep inside the torrent of words racing through her mind. "I just don't want to upset you if I don't find my cat."

Knox leaned toward her, his heavenly scent wrapping her senses. "You can't upset me, Miranda."

Miranda looked at the little cottage with cats painted along the door. Old Farm Cat Rescue was written on a hanger and there were two cats sitting in the window. Knox put in the application. He got her approved.

The air in the car was thick and for just a moment Miranda wondered if he was going to say *I love you*.

Her soul craved the words but when he squeezed her hand, she knew the moment had passed.

Which of course it had. They'd been together, officially, less than a month. One did not just shout out *I love you* after so little time. And what would she have even said if he'd said the words?

Miranda knew the answer with more certainty than she'd felt in forever. Her heart recognized his. Knox was the person she wanted to talk to first in the morning and last before her eyes slipped into slumber. He was the one she wanted beside her.

She'd fallen for him. Maybe years ago when they were competing. Or maybe in the weeks since she'd returned. Either way, she loved him.

"Let's go meet some kitty cats." Miranda opened the door, hesitated for a moment then pulled her hand away from his and grabbed the soft carrier. She didn't have to come home with a cat. But taking it with her was a good omen and she was using that.

The entry of the rescue smelled like cat—but in a good way. There were kittens in several kennels on the wall and a door with a bubble letter sign reading *Cat Room—Fluff Guaranteed!*

An older white woman stood, her eyes trained on Knox. "I'm Kitty Resen. Yes. My parents named me Kitty. No, I don't think that is the only reason that I started a cat rescue. Yes, I do see the irony. Yes, I get these questions a lot."

"I bet." Knox held out a hand, offering Kitty his winning smile.

The older woman put her free hand over her chest as she shook his hand. "My, my, you are a gorgeous young man. Quite the keeper." She winked at Miranda.

"Hear that, Miranda? I'm a keeper."

"You are, and he'll be bragging on that all afternoon Ms. Resen." Miranda gave a playful exasperated noise.

"First time in my life I've ever been called a keeper. You better believe I'm going to brag on it." Knox was grinning but she could see the hint of pride, too.

It probably was the first time. He rarely talked about his time in foster care. But his reaction to Leo, Ben and their mother was seared in her memory. His need to walk away after, his withdrawal.

"You are very much a keeper, Knox." She reached for his hand and squeezed it.

Kitty sighed. "Well, you seem thoroughly taken, young man. But if she cuts you free…" She wagged a finger and laughed.

"You'll be my first stop, ma'am."

"All right, let's get to the real reason you're here." Kitty clapped her hands, turning her full attention to Miranda. "A cat for you, my dear."

If she spoke, Miranda worried she might say she was just looking. Or something that would make

Kitty realize she wasn't the best choice for a cat. So she nodded and held her breath.

Kitty picked up a piece of paper and read over it. "Surgeon—fancy. Not home at regular hours but able to keep water and food out all the time. Do you plan to declaw?"

"Oh, no." Miranda didn't keep up with much veterinary medicine but as a cat lover she'd seen the studies on declawing. It was detrimental to a cat's mental health and their longevity. They had to relearn how to walk and she doubted the rescue would allow an adopter to adopt who said yes.

"Right answer." Kitty tapped her nose. "Do you mind an adult cat?"

"No." As cute as kittens were, she didn't think she had the right home for one. "I think my home is better suited for an adult cat."

Kitty wrote a few things on the adoption paperwork. "How do you feel about one that is a little more aloof?" Kitty looked at Miranda and she could tell there was a specific feline that she was thinking of.

"As long as the cat likes me, aloof works. After all, the cat will be alone, sometimes for almost twelve hours."

"Right." Kitty sat the paper down. "I think you are perfect for one of the cats. Assuming she likes you."

Miranda's stomach turned as Kitty led them into a meet-and-greet room. There were cat toys on the floor and pillows for her and Knox to sit on. "What if the cat doesn't like me? She said she had one. One cat that fit me. Maybe this wasn't the best idea."

"Sweetie, take a deep breath." Knox inhaled and waited for Miranda to follow. "If the cat doesn't like you there are others. Their website literally has twenty. And if you don't find one today, well, it's nearly always kitten season. More will come. You can't fail this."

You can't fail this. Miranda latched on to the words. He was right. There was no way to crash and burn on meeting a rescue cat.

"I think another massage may be in order tonight." Knox kissed her cheek.

"Maybe. Your fingers are super delicious."

The door opened on the last phrase and heat flooded Miranda's cheeks. "Oh, uh—"

"No need to apologize for young love. Despite my flirtations I still remember what it was like when my Harold and I were together before he departed this level of existence."

"Young love." Knox hit Miranda's side. "Did you hear that?"

Miranda held her breath. She had heard it. *Love.*

"Young." Knox grinned.

"Right." Miranda's throat was tight. Of course he was talking about the word *young.* Getting older was weird. At forty she didn't feel old.

There were more lines around her eyes, and her back ached in the morning. Society noticed, too.

The few times she'd logged in to a dating app most of her potential matches were men in their sixties.

Before she could think too much on the young love comment, Kitty opened the carrier and a bright white cat with brilliant green eyes hopped out, turned and promptly glared at Kitty then walked past Miranda and Knox, twitching its tail.

"Meet Icy."

Icy twitched her tail but didn't turn when Kitty said her name.

"I take it the name is due to personality." Miranda held out her hand, surprised when Icy sniffed it then let her run her hand on the top of her head.

"I would love to tell you that it's because of her color, and if I was prone to lying I might." Kitty let out a chuckle. "But honestly, I am a little surprised she's letting you touch her like that. Typically, she runs into the corner."

Icy's bright eyes focused on Miranda. She tilted her head, and Miranda could see the cat weighing her options.

Miranda ran her finger under the cat's chin and the creature let out a soft purr. The rumble was gone in an instant. "Can't change that it came out Icy." Miranda winked at the cat, knowing the girl didn't understand. The animal may not speak her language, but she could hear Miranda's happy tone.

Icy let out a meow then climbed into Miranda's lap. The cat turned three times then settled down, laying her head on Miranda's knee.

"I think you have a cat." Knox chuckled as he held his hand up. Icy sniffed it, then let him rub her ears.

"I think y'all have a cat." Kitty sighed.

Miranda's ears were buzzing on Kitty's words that she almost missed her next statement. "I love filling out adoption paperwork." The older woman clapped, ignoring Icy's glare. "You'll take her with you today?"

"I will." Miranda kept her gaze focused on Kitty. If she looked at Knox, she'd look for all the ways he might be reacting to Kitty's comment on *them* getting a cat.

So many thoughts, questions and hopes hung on that statement. He hadn't corrected Kitty. Knox also hadn't confirmed it. After all, pointing out that it wasn't their cat would be uncomfortable for Kitty—and maybe them, too.

"You are going to be so spoiled, Icy." Knox kissed Miranda's cheek and stood. His posture was relaxed, his face beaming. The man was aware of what he'd accomplished, and she doubted he'd stop crowing about it for at least the next week.

"You'd think we were torturing her!" Knox opened Miranda's door as Icy screamed bloody murder in the cat carrier.

"I think she thinks we are torturing her." Miranda rushed toward the laundry room. "I want to release her by the litter box so she knows where it is."

"I'll order dinner." Knox moved to the kitchen and found Miranda's stack of takeout menus. It was in nearly the same location as his. And he already knew what she preferred at most of the locations.

They'd slipped into this so fast. Yet, it felt—perfect. When Kitty had called them *young love*, he'd wondered if his feelings for Miranda were so easy to see. He loved her. Though sitting across the floor from her at a cat rescue was hardly the place to make such an announcement.

So he'd joked about the word *young*. And her face had fallen just a touch. Or he thought it had; maybe he was just imagining things. Everything was tumbled together in a puzzle that made no sense but was perfection.

Whether it happened in the past few weeks or years ago when they were competing with each other, he wasn't sure.

And it didn't matter.

"She's inspecting her new kingdom." Miranda stepped behind him, wrapping her arms around his waist and laying her head against his shoulder. "Thank you. She is perfect."

"She likes you. That's what matters." Knox kissed the top of her head as he pulled out three menus for her to choose from.

Miranda squeezed him. "She likes you, too. Maybe not as much as me, but you are well passed tolerating."

"Maybe before I pushed her butt into the carrier." Icy had screeched and Miranda had been using her soft voice, trying to calm her. The cat may not have obliged but it was clear Icy blamed him not Miranda.

"She'll forgive you." Miranda kissed his cheek, more hope showing in her eyes than Knox thought right.

"Hmm." Knox doubted Icy was the forgiving kind. Hopefully, once she was fully settled in, she'd remember she tolerated him at the rescue once upon a time.

Miranda tapped the menu for the Italian place. "I feel like lasagna. And their portions are big enough I'll have leftovers for tomorrow."

"What if we order the family size and we can eat it for a few days?" The question was out of his mouth before Knox could think through the implications. He'd just invited himself to stay...for a few days.

His mind wandered to the ways he could pull the words back but his heart refused to say them. He wanted to be here. When he wasn't at Hope, with Miranda was where he wanted to be.

"That sounds like a good plan." She moved to the fridge, grabbing a bottle of white wine.

It was such a small moment. One they'd hopefully do thousands more times. But it felt monumental.

Knox quickly ordered on a delivery app, then accepted the wineglass.

Icy wandered from the laundry room, her gaze taking in her new surroundings. Her tail twitched as she walked past them. And he swore she'd glared at him.

"I guess she approves of her new domain?" Miranda tipped her wineglass toward the cat. "Right?"

"Based on her reaction to the cat carrier, I think we'd know if she didn't." We. Two little letters. One little pronoun. All containing a world of possibilities.

"When you said you did something, this was not what I thought you meant. Not in any universe, but I'm glad you filled out the application for me, Knox. Thank you." Miranda's gaze was focused on Icy, who was sniffing around the couch in the other room like she owned it.

"What did you think I meant?" Knox took a sip of the wine. It was drier than he typically preferred but had a good body.

"I figured you wanted to talk about Hugh's job. I swear everyone is trying to get me to put in for it. Hugh was as pushy as I've ever seen him. Dr. O'Sullivan made a comment about me being his main competition—he is so sure of himself." She tsked her tongue. "What is it with bone bros?"

The rest of what she was saying was lost on him. He could see her lips moving, knew there was more, but his brain had locked down. No one had talked to him about putting in. Jackson had made a random statement about it, but no one else. Not even Hugh. He'd assumed that people weren't seriously talking replacements yet.

But they were.

They just weren't talking to him.

No. He had to have misunderstood. There had to be a mistake. "Hugh spoke to you?" He'd stayed at Hope. He'd been there the longest. He had the certs. Knox was good at his job.

No, Knox was damn great at his job.

"Yes."

His fingers tingled as Miranda squeezed his hand. This wasn't right.

"Has he not talked to you?" Her dark gaze held what he knew was the truth. She wasn't surprised he hadn't talked to Knox.

That was a bigger blow than Hugh not speaking with him.

"Don't pretend, Miranda." Knox set his wineglass down. He needed to do something. Something...but he wasn't sure what.

Setting her glass beside his, Miranda pressed herself against him, hugging him tightly. "Knox, take a breath."

He didn't want to follow her command, but he did. The air filling his lungs was tinged with the sweet scent he'd come to think of as hers. Instead of calming him, it drew frustration.

Why had she not talked about this with him?

Why was she not plotting the competition? It would be friendlier now. But this was what they thrived on.

Because she doesn't think I'm competition.

The truth slammed his chest. What had happened? He was better than he'd been before. So much better. And he was still coming in second... or rather last.

"I should be a top candidate." Knox tapped his fingers against the counter. His whole body was vibrating.

Miranda's hands pressed on either side of his cheeks. "Look at me."

His gaze focused on her before he leaned his forehead against hers. "Why has no one talked to me?"

"Because you aren't a top candidate for the board." The soft words were hammers to his soul.

"That isn't fair." He pulled back, his body wanting to flee, his heart wanting comfort, his mind wanting answers. "And it can't be true. I'm accomplished. I have all the certs. I've been at Hope longer than anyone besides Hugh."

"It's that last one that's the issue. The board wants a 'well-rounded' candidate. One with a few hospitals on their résumé. Loyalty deducts points, not adds them." Miranda crossed her arms and shrugged. "You were right the first time. It's not fair. But life isn't fair."

Life isn't fair.

How he hated that phrase. Hated how everyone

accepted and how there was nothing he could do to change that.

"I know that, Miranda." Knox pushed a hand through his hair, not caring that the motion was too rough and a few hairs came loose from his head—not pain-free.

He closed his eyes, trying to gain some bearing. "I grew up in the system. I didn't have a loving home. Parents who encouraged me. Sisters who had my back. I didn't have the advantage you and others had."

"I didn't grow up in the system but I didn't have a loving home, Knox."

"Not a competition, Miranda." He choked back a sob. "Sorry. I know you had it rough in a different way. I know that." This wasn't her fault. Nothing she was saying was wrong. It simply wasn't what he wanted to hear.

At least not right now.

"I need to leave." He grabbed his keys off the table and moved to kiss her cheek, hating how rigid she was. "It's not about you. It's me. I need a night. I'm sorry."

"Stay."

The word hit his back and he paused. "I feel like I am coming out of my skin, Miranda. I just need a night." He kept moving toward the door, waiting for her to call out again. But the word never came.

CHAPTER FOURTEEN

"THINK THE FAMILY-SIZE platter was a universal joke?" Miranda asked Icy as she cut a square for her breakfast and placed another in her lunch box. Getting a chance to eat on shift was hardly guaranteed, but she could always eat it cold.

Icy flipped her tail and then walked out of the kitchen.

Miranda reached for her cell phone for at least the hundredth time since Knox walked out last night. She'd typed so many messages and deleted all of them. He'd wanted time to process.

She understood that. She agreed with him. It was a crappy thing to not at least talk to him. She knew in Hugh's mind Knox should be a top candidate. But Hugh wasn't on the board. And the board liked to brag about doctors from "high profile" hospitals choosing Hope.

Longevity should be rewarded. And when it wasn't going to happen, Hugh should discuss it. Talk to Knox about his options so they could chart his next move.

Being hurt was a natural emotion. But they weren't competitors anymore. She wasn't even applying. This was what partners helped each other with.

Lance never discussed his plans with her. Just

delivered the news of his latest new job with divorce papers. Her parents showed little emotion in their union. United in making their daughters, and themselves, as great as possible, no matter the consequences.

Miranda had little experience in this, but she knew what she wanted. A partnership that shared. There were several hospitals in the local area if Knox wanted to move on. Or he could accept his role at Hope. Maybe it didn't come with a fancy title and a few more dollars an hour pay, but it did come with more free time. Assuming he took it.

"What should I tell him?" Miranda held the phone up to Icy, who did not bother to look at it on her way to the laundry room. "Not helpful."

The cat twitched her tail but didn't offer anything.

Miranda looked at her watch; time to get going. "I'll see you when I'm home," she called after the white floof whose tail had just rounded the corner cabinet. "One day with a cat and I am already talking to her."

Miranda looked at her phone one more time then slid it into her backpack. She'd see Knox at the hospital. Hopefully by then she'd know the perfect thing to say.

"Miranda!" Knox's voice was bright and airy as it called across the parking garage.

That was not what she'd expected.

"Knox." Miranda smiled as he placed a quick kiss on her cheek. "So you're better?"

"Much. And I am so sorry, sweetie. I shouldn't have left like that and I absolutely should not have compared our childhoods. That was a terrible thing. I am sorry."

She wrapped an arm around his waist, some of the tension leaking from her. "You said you were sorry twice."

"Is that not enough? Do you want a third sorry?" Knox pressed his lips to her head as they waited for the elevator.

She playfully pushed her elbow into his ribs. "You know that isn't necessary. Are you doing better?"

"Yep." Knox used his free hand to tap his head. "Cause I have a plan."

His eyes were bright but his body tensed on the words. She'd seen this Knox. Worked beside him for years. The competitive man was here now. Except this wasn't a prize he could win.

"Knox."

"I'm applying, Miranda. I will make the board tell me I'm not the best candidate. From this moment on, I will be one of Patrick O'Sullivan's top competitors."

"All right." Miranda suspected he'd make it to the final round, if just for looks. But if this was what he needed, then she'd support it.

"It also means I'm going to put in extra shifts."

Ah, the unwritten "rules of the game." Extra shifts might not be explicitly stated as a necessity, but anyone currently on staff who wanted to throw their name in the ring would be expected to live at the hospital as much as possible.

"Not sure that is actually possible, Knox." The man was already pushing all the hours he was legally allowed to work most weeks.

The real reward for good work was more work. Not promotions. Not recognition. Just asking you to deliver more than you already were.

No matter how hard she'd pushed herself at her old hospitals, it hadn't resulted in anything more than an increased workload. And when she'd broken under the system, they'd pushed her work off on another high performer. Restarting the cycle.

Knox tapped his foot. There were words dancing around his brain. She could practically see them forming in his mind. But none escaped.

"You already work the maximum hours."

"I've stepped back over the last two weeks." He pushed the button for the elevator, like forcing the number the second time would make the thing magically appear.

Miranda leaned her head against his shoulder, weighing the different paths she could take here. If Knox wanted to put in, he should. Would the hospital board interview him? Almost certainly. Would they select him? Almost certainly not.

"Two weeks of one less shift is not slowing

down, Knox. Not really." She doubted anyone even really noticed.

"I also plan to talk to Hugh about why he didn't talk to me."

That was a good plan. Hugh had chickened out on this one. Calling him out on it wasn't a terrible thing. Knox had deserved more, and standing up for that was good.

"So. When do we start the competition?" The elevator doors opened, and Knox stepped on.

"We don't." Miranda wasn't interested in the competition. Not anymore. And she really wasn't interested in it with her boyfriend. She'd support him with the application. Listen to any strategy he wanted to put out there. But she had no intention of putting in.

Knox hit her hip with his. "I know you had a bad time before, but you should put in. If I have to lose to anyone, I'd rather lose to you. At least I know how to do that."

"Knox." Miranda pulled at the back of her neck. She knew he meant it as a joke. Their past was them competing. Challenging each other. It had made them better surgeons. She believed that deep in her core. But over the past month they'd become partners.

That was a blissful state she had no desire to upset with competition.

"Miranda." He put his hands on his hips. "I'm serious. You are perfect for it."

Perfect. Knox's words radiated in her. He thought she should put in. Perhaps she should at least consider it.

"I appreciate that. I really do. But I like my life here. I've rebuilt my relationship with my sisters. I like Hope. I have what I want here. I'm happy. It's enough for me. And now, because of my very sweet boyfriend, I have a cat."

"So, tell me how Icy is."

She appreciated the shift in conversation. Icy was something she doubted she'd ever tire of talking about. "We made it through the night just fine."

The elevator doors opened, and Hugh was standing just outside them. "Good morning, Miranda. Knox, do you have a minute?"

"I do." Knox crossed his arms then uncrossed them as he stepped off the elevator.

"Good luck." Miranda whispered the words under her breath, not sure who needed it more.

"I am surprised you didn't want to talk to me sooner." Knox heard the frustration in his voice. Maybe that wasn't a fair way to start off the conversation but it was all he could muster in the moment.

Hugh looked at his feet, his gaze hovering on the floor.

Knox waited a second then let out a breath. Hugh was his mentor. A man who'd believed in him. Counseling him when he needed it, comforting him on days that felt like the end of the world. He didn't deserve Knox's frustration. "I didn't mean that."

"I think you did." Hugh crossed his arms, then finally met Knox's gaze. "I knew you'd ask about putting in."

"Oh, I'm putting in." Knox was qualified. Maybe the board wouldn't choose him, but that didn't mean he couldn't make them consider him. And if they considered him—well, Knox was nearly certain he could win the position.

The tips of Hugh's lips turned down and a pit opened in Knox's belly.

"Take a walk with me." Hugh started moving down the hallway without waiting for Knox to reply.

He caught up quickly. "You don't think I've got a shot?"

"I don't."

The words may as well have been hammers. Or knives. Tiny bullets shattering the self-confidence Knox prided himself on.

"I am a damn fine surgeon."

"I know." Hugh shook his head as he opened the door to the hospital courtyard. Or what the hospital claimed was its courtyard. There were a few flowerpots, currently missing any flowers, and some uncomfortable benches. But at least the sun was shining and no one else would hear whatever his mentor had to say. "You are a great surgeon, Knox. But the board doesn't really care about that."

"How could they not?" He was great in the surgical suite. Great at bedside. Great with the irritable parents, spouses, kids of parents. He was great at his job. How could that just not matter, according to Hugh?

"You've only ever worked at Hope."

"That should make me the top guy. I'm the expert." Knox couldn't seem to stop interrupting. He felt like he had all those years ago in state care. How many times had he been told his best wasn't good enough? He'd done everything he was supposed to. This wasn't the way his story was supposed to go.

Knox grabbed his phone and pulled up the emails he'd gotten this morning. "I reactivated my online job portal less than twelve hours ago. I have two hospitals and a headhunter reaching out. In *twelve* hours." Others wanted him. Why not Hope?

Hugh stopped in the small circle in the center of the "garden." The word *breathe* was carved into the stone. A reminder that once upon a time someone planned for this area to be used more. A plan that had not come to fruition.

"My position is more than cutting." Hugh held up his hand, but Knox had run out of words to interrupt. "It's admin. It's fundraising. It's training interns. It's mentoring." Hugh held up his hand, ticking off the list of things he did.

Knox could do all those things. Knox had done all those things.

Hugh laid a hand on Knox's shoulder. "You could do all those things. Have done them."

It was like he was reading Knox's thoughts. If only Knox could do the same, he might understand why his mentor seemed to be saying he was the perfect fit and yet not even a candidate.

"But…" Knox held up his hands. This would be easier if Hugh would just drop the hammer.

Instead, his mentor bit his lip and looked over his shoulder.

Knox knew this moment. He'd seen it in caseworkers who were trying to find a way to lessen the blow they were about to deliver. The truth was that hard news was always hard, no matter how you said it.

"Just say it." Knox pulled his hand along his face.

"You haven't left and that is the problem. Leaving broadens your networking ability. It means there are candidates who will have colleagues around the nation."

"I have that, too." Maybe not to the same level, but in the local area, he knew everyone. Literally.

"So I'm going to be punished for loyalty? Where exactly is it written that I have to have worked in multiple hospitals to get this promotion?" He pushed his hands into his pockets, then pulled them out. He needed to be professional but his brain also wanted to revert to the scared kid he'd been once upon a time. The one who'd yelled that life wasn't fair. That had believed if he just worked hard enough there was no ladder too high to climb.

"Unwritten rules are often more important than others. You know this."

He did. His childhood was a list of unwritten rules. Constantly changing ones, too. This family didn't like it if you ate a snack without asking; that family got mad if you asked too many times for snacks when you could just grab them from the pantry. Silly little things that didn't matter in the real world. That didn't change who he was as a person.

Working in other hospitals didn't make Miranda or anyone else a better doctor. Having worked at Hope his whole career didn't make him less qualified. But on paper one was better than the other. For reasons.

Reasons that meant nothing. Even if Hugh could explain them right now they would mean nothing. They were reasons to score someone. And once more he was being found lacking.

"I'm still putting in." Let them tell him no. Let the committee look at his résumé; his work, and tell him no.

"If you decide you want a reference for another hospital, I'd be happy to give you one. I think you would make an excellent head of surgery. And I think it's unfair that your long tenure here will be held against you by the board."

A reference to leave. Not a reference for the position.

Miranda walked past the courtyard. Even through the glass, he could see the concern in her body language. Was she looking for him? Or concerned for a patient? Both?

"You told Miranda to apply." He hadn't meant to say that. But may as well lay all the cards on the table.

"I did." Hugh took a deep breath, then looked at his watch. They needed to wrap this up. There were patients to tend to and surgeries to handle. "I think she would make an excellent head surgeon."

"And I would, too, just not here." Knox blew out a breath, then looked at his own watch. He wasn't going to accomplish anything else with this. And he appreciated Hugh's candor. Still, there had to be a way. He just hadn't figured it out yet. "Thanks, Hugh."

The older man nodded and tapped his shoulder a few times. Knox hoped the gesture was born of kindness but part of him feared it was pity.

He looked at the emails. One hospital in Nevada, another in Maine, and the headhunter told him he had openings in four states. He looked at his watch one more time, then sent three emails. It didn't hurt to at least talk to them.

What did he have to lose?

CHAPTER FIFTEEN

"YOU REALLY AREN'T interested in putting in for the position?" Olive's youngest daughter was on Miranda's hip as her mother pulled the cookies Miranda had asked for from her bag. Her sister's home bakery had grown by leaps and bounds over the past year. Living close enough to get fresh deliveries was definitely a perk.

"Nope." Miranda jiggled Rose, enjoying the one-year-old's laugh.

"I am worried about Knox, though." The statement was out, and she regretted it. He looked broken when she'd seen him in the garden with Hugh. But he wouldn't talk to her about what was said on their short breaks.

Just waved away her concern. Tonight she wanted him to talk to her.

"What's wrong with Knox?" Olive raised a brow as she pulled the lid off the cookies.

Miranda leaned over the box as her face heated. He'd had an understandably bad reaction to a bad situation. He was stressed and this was their problem, one she wanted to discuss with him, not someone else, even her sister.

"Those look so pretty." The chocolate cookies had ribbons of white through them. "Did you put white chocolate in these?"

Knox loved chocolate cookies. These were her *I know you had a bad day and I want to hash out next steps* cookies. It was a new category, one she hoped not to use very often. Though any excuse for Olive's cookies was a good one.

"It's marshmallow. These are my hot cocoa cookies. I'm planning to make batches for Christmas. This is test number four. I do need your and Knox's honest opinion please. Now, answer my question, Miranda. What's up with Knox?"

Her sister put her hands on her hips. The same motion she'd seen so often growing up as her little sister took on their parents. Olive was the one who'd never cared what their parents said. She'd wanted to be a baker.

Miranda was a doctor; Kelly, her middle sister, a lawyer. Olive was meant to be the CEO. And in many ways she was. Her bakery was doing well, but it wasn't the penthouse suite her parents had wanted for her.

"He isn't a candidate for the head surgeon position. Not really." Miranda handed Rose back as the toddler reached for Olive.

"That sucks." Olive put her hand on Rose's mouth as the little one started to repeat the word. "That is just for Mommy, Rosie."

Rose didn't really understand words other than mama and daddy and no, yet. But she was becoming a real parrot. Miranda needed to watch herself around the little ones now, too.

"It does. And he won't talk about it." Miranda took a deep breath and recounted how he left the other night. "Walked out, like Lance."

"Did he?" Her sister dropped a kiss on her daughter's nose then looked back at Miranda. Her eyes held a statement that she didn't say. Sisters.

"I want a partnership. I can help him. If he'll let me." She'd run him through interview questions. Make sure meals were packed for his long shifts. Hold him when it got overwhelming and when the job went to someone else.

"If he won't let me…" Her voice caught. Not sure she wanted to travel down that path.

"One bad night and you are already worrying? Wow, Miranda. Take a deep breath."

"Take a deep breath? That all you got? Not super helpful advice, sis." Miranda stuck out her tongue—something Olive had done repeatedly as a kid. Her sister was right, though.

Which, based on her sister's expression, she was well aware of.

"I'm the little sister. The oldest is the one who is supposed to have all the answers."

The door to her town house opened and Knox stepped in. His eyes went to Olive and Rose before he went over and kissed Miranda. "I'm Knox." He held his hand out to Olive.

"You weren't kidding. He is hot." Olive winked

at Miranda, clearly enjoying the horror she knew was on her face.

"Olive is my youngest sister. She takes great pride in being the baby of the family." Miranda didn't stick her tongue out again, but she wanted to.

"Enjoy the cookies." Olive waved. "It was nice to meet you, Knox."

"You, too."

Olive squeezed Rose. "Time for us to head home, Rosie. Think about what I said, Miranda." Then she headed out.

"Cookies?" Knox kissed the top of her head.

Good. Better for him to focus on that than Olive's parting shot.

"I thought you might like some cookies after shift." Miranda pulled away and headed for the kitchen to grab the cookies. "Olive wants our thoughts on these hot cocoa cookies."

Miranda handed him one, but Knox didn't look as thrilled at the cookies as she'd expected. "Do you not like chocolate cookies anymore?"

"I love chocolate cookies, and I'm stunned you remembered that."

He and Jackson had joked about Knox's obsession with chocolate during his residency. Jackson had even playfully kept chocolate bars in his locker and thrown one at Knox anytime he was off. Telling him to eat it and become himself again.

The running joke hadn't happened since she'd returned. But back then they were exhausted residents operating on caffeine and adrenaline. Work balance had shifted in the past few years. Med students got breaks, not enough, but more than they'd had. The grueling hours to become a surgeon still meant people were hungry more than they often realized on shift.

"I remember a lot about our residency." Miranda grabbed her own cookie. "We were constantly together. I don't think this—" she waved a hand between them "—would have worked then. But maybe." There was no way to know for sure.

They'd been competitors but not enemies. Maybe even then the spark had been there.

"I…" Knox hesitated. He looked from the cookie to her. "I almost want to say no. Because if it would have worked then—" he reached for her hand "—then we lost years."

Years… Miranda's heart nearly exploded. Years. A single word with so much meaning. If they'd lost years, it meant he felt they had years together. "We have now."

"We do." He leaned over, his lips meeting hers. He tasted of chocolate and fun. His body molded to hers. "And right now, I am taking you to bed."

There were things to discuss. His day. The conversation with Hugh. The unspoken *I love you* she felt hovering in her heart. But it was impossible to focus when his lips were on hers and his thumb was tracing her nipple through her cotton shirt.

Maybe putting it off wasn't the best idea, but they had time. Lots of time.

She put the rest of her cookie on the counter. "Knox." His name on her lips felt so right.

He lifted her, carrying her to the bedroom.

Knox ran his hand over Icy's head as he grabbed two more cookies and glasses of milk. Miranda was pulling up a television show. A night in after his rough talk with Hugh was exactly what the doctor ordered. Miranda was a mind reader.

"These cookies are amazing." Knox set the plate on the table by Miranda's couch.

"I figured they were the perfect way to end a tough day." She stretched, the T-shirt she was wearing lifting to show her stomach...where his lips had trailed just an hour or so before.

But it was her words that caught his attention. Tough day.

Their patients today had all had standard outcomes. Everyone would recover. It was the kind of day everyone wished for. There was no reason for him to have a tough day...except for his conversation with Hugh.

He hadn't told her what Hugh had said. Yes, he'd been frustrated that Hugh had spoken to Miranda, and everyone else he thought was a candidate. But today's conversation could have been Hugh telling Knox that he was the top candidate. That he'd told everyone to put in because it looked good.

Part of him had hoped Hugh might say he hadn't thought it necessary to talk to him. Because of course Knox would put in and be competitive.

"You knew Hugh would tell me he didn't think I was competitive for the position." His blood cooled.

"I told you that the other night." Miranda's dark eyes held his as she tilted her head. "You've been at Hope too long. You need to move on if you want that role."

I put in for two jobs this afternoon.

Those words ping-ponged in his mind but he didn't say them. The job in Maine was for a lead general surgeon with pediatric oncology credits and HR had sent a follow-up email almost immediately. It was nice to be wanted.

But he kept those words buried. No sense rushing any more than he already had. Rage applying for a new position was one thing; actually considering a whole other.

"So you got me pity cookies?" He closed his eyes, took a deep breath. He wasn't mad at Miranda. There was no reason to take his frustration out on her. "I'm sorry."

"These aren't pity cookies. These are delicious chocolate cookies."

He raised a brow and she shrugged.

"Fine. Maybe they are a little bit pity cookies. But they are commiserating pity cookies. Because I agree you should be competitive for the job."

Miranda laid her hand on his chest as he sat down. "It should only matter how well you cut, how you deal with patients and how you manage. All things you're great at."

"They are good pity cookies." Knox kissed the top of her head, trying to push away the feelings in his belly. None of this was Miranda's fault. "But I am not ready to admit defeat just yet."

"Help me plot the best strategy to make the board rue the day they didn't consider me a top candidate?" Maybe he didn't have a shot. But Knox Peters had been down a lot in his life and always came out on top…or damn close to it. No reason for this to be different.

CHAPTER SIXTEEN

"So, I THINK Dr. O'Sullivan will crash and burn in his interview. He is so sure he's the best for the position that there is no way he is prepping the way he should. That's good news. The bad news is I was able to confirm that Leah Kilio from Southland is applying." Knox didn't even look up from the tablet that seemed attached to his hands the past week as he walked up to her by the elevator bank.

If he was not seeing a patient or consulting this seemed to be all he thought of. If he was like this during their residency, she'd not seen it. The man was working constantly and tracking whatever he could regarding the job opening otherwise. And she doubted it was going to make a difference.

And was he even enjoying this? Did he want it that badly or was it only because he'd been told he wasn't a top candidate?

Miranda had done so many things she didn't want to. Done them because she thought that was what was expected of her. And it led to soul-crushing burnout. And Knox was headed down that path.

"Why do you want this job?" The question was out before she'd really contemplated it. But she wanted an answer.

"Miranda?" Knox laid his hand over hers as his tablet dinged.

"What was that?"

"Nothing. Just an email." Knox turned his tablet over and leaned a little closer.

A twinge raced down her spine but she took a deep breath. It was an email and she wanted to focus on the job.

"Do you really want this job? Or do you just think you should want it?" Miranda watched his features, saw the tightening in his lips, the appearance of tiny lines around his eyes. Nothing about what he was doing appeared to be for fun.

Grabbing his tablet Knox tapped a few things out then flipped it around. "My résumé is fantastic."

That wasn't an answer.

"I think we should take a night off from all the prep." Before he could argue, she held up a hand. "Just a night. Some rest and relaxation." Miranda winked, but knew he didn't see it. All his attention was focused on the tablet she was beginning to truly hate.

Pulling the tablet to her, she pulled up the calendar app. "Schedule some downtime."

"Downtime? What do you mean? This is prime prep time. Dr. O'Sullivan is already working all the shifts he legally can."

And he's grouchy as can be about it.

Miranda kept that observation to herself. She

was not derailing this conversation by talking about Patrick. He'd made his choice. She hoped he was happy no matter the outcome. If she had to work for him it would be fine.

Not as good as Hugh. But then those were shoes whoever got the position would need to grow into.

"I want downtime from this." She tapped the tablet and rolled her eyes and he pulled it away, correcting whatever she'd just messed up.

"We don't know when the interviews will start."

Miranda grabbed his wrist. "But we do know they will be after the position is posted. Which to date, it is not. You cannot apply for a position that is not open. So I ask again. Can we schedule some time for us? Just the two of us?"

"How will Icy feel about that?" Knox leaned over; his mouth was so close that if they weren't at the hospital she'd close the distance.

"Icy will insert herself as she sees fit." Miranda chuckled. The cat was very comfortable in her new role as empress of the condo.

Knox looked at the tablet. She could see him wanting to argue. He was so focused, so intent. But it felt like a war to prove he belonged, rather than a battle for something he truly wanted.

Or maybe I'm putting my feelings on this.

"Knox? Downtime?"

"Of course." He nodded his head, but there was a look in his eyes.

Her hip buzzed. A distraction!

The joy was immediately tempered by reality. A consult for the ER meant someone was having a terrible day.

"I'm needed downstairs." Miranda squeezed his hand. "Schedule it." Then she turned and headed for the elevator bank.

Part of her couldn't shake the idea that he didn't really want it. If he did, he'd have left Hope. It was admirable that he'd stayed, providing continuity for patients and staff alike. But Knox knew what it took to advance past certain levels. Corporate medicine wasn't ideal, but it was the life that physicians lived too often.

That was something they should talk about. But how?

And her brain refused to provide any answers on the short elevator ride down to the ER.

"Dr. Paulson." Dr. Hinks raised a hand; the smile on his face made her uneasy.

"You paged me?"

"Yes, I have a consult in bay four. The man is in his eighties, got into a motorcycle accident." Dr. Hinks rolled his eyes then caught himself and cleared his throat.

So the tendency to judge his patients hadn't miraculously fixed itself over the past six weeks. Shame.

"I ordered the CT and MRI scans. They are loaded. Looks to be a bleeder in the stomach. Maybe a burst ulcer. He's pretty beat up."

"A motorcycle accident will do that." Miranda grabbed a tablet from the charging station and pulled up the results. Clifford Douglass, eighty-one. Motorcycle accident. Broken right wrist. Bruised ribs. Contusion on cheek. No concussion, thank you, helmets. What looked to be a bleeding ulcer in the stomach.

She pulled up the scans and saw the notes that he'd been seen by gastro for symptoms eight weeks ago. The bleeding looked about the same. But no worse.

"Let me go take a look." Miranda started for the door, but Dr. Hinks stepped in front of her. "Yes?"

"I was wondering if you knew who might be putting in for Dr. Lawton's position—I was thinking of cross training and just wanted to wish people luck."

Wanted to find out who to suck up to was more like it. If Dr. Hinks wanted to figure out who to schmooze, he'd have to do it himself.

"I have a patient with internal bleeding. That takes priority." She moved around him and knocked on the patient's door before entering the room. "Mr. Douglass. I'm Dr. Paulson. Nice to meet you."

"Call me Clifford, please. You'll excuse me if I don't say the same." The older white man chuckled then grabbed his side. "Boy, you never realize how much you don't want to feel your ribs until you have to feel your ribs."

"That might be the truest statement about those bones as I've ever heard." Miranda smiled and offered the man her hand. "So you were on a motorcycle?"

Clifford shook his head and sighed. "Let me guess, you can't believe someone my age would even bother."

"I never said that. Motorcycles are…" She patched too many people together after an accident to have a ready platitude.

"For young people."

"No. I would say they are for no one." Miranda gestured to Clifford. "You have the bruises and injuries to show why I think that. Age has nothing to do with it. But I am not here to talk broken bones and achy ribs."

She tapped a few things on the tablet and watched the television screen light up with Clifford's MRI. It hadn't been looking for the ulcer but all the indicators were there.

"I think you have an ulcer. And it's bleeding."

"Its name is Bertha."

Miranda blinked, opened her mouth but didn't quite manage to make any sounds.

Clifford hit his belly in the upper right quadrant where the ulcer was located. "She and I have been friends for at least three years according to my gastro doc. Nice man. Very interested in my fiber intake. Did an endoscopy to confirm a few weeks ago."

Miranda smiled and nodded. All physician specialties had certain traits and it was funny when patients picked up on them, too.

"That annoying lady is why I was on the motorcycle." Clifford glared at the screen.

Now she was truly lost.

"I'm sorry. What?"

Clifford chuckled and his face showed the instant regret. "I spent my whole life in the office. Always going for the next big promotion. Hell, I'm not even sure why. To prove I could. To make more money—had enough."

He cleared his throat and closed his eyes. The room was silent for a moment before he reopened them and smiled. A grin Miranda was sure he didn't feel.

"Bertha has probably been with me for a decade or so. Though she got super angry about a year ago. That was when I actually got help for the constant feelings of exhaustion. So I could work more."

The elderly man closed his eyes and a tear slipped down them. "So I could work more. What a statement to make. My kids don't talk to me and my ex-wife. Well, she hasn't picked up the phone in nearly thirty years. I demonstrated that work was more important than everything else and they took that lesson to heart."

Miranda nodded. It wasn't as uncommon of a story as one wanted to believe. Elderly people were often without family. Some of that was because family was too busy to deal with the effects of age. But some of it was because the person hadn't given attention or love to others when they'd needed it.

"Anyways. I understand why I am alone. I accept the choices I made. I can't change them. But I can change myself. So yeah. That is Bertha. My ulcer. The thing that finally got me out of the office. It seems small, but I didn't want my only accomplishment to be the thing my family left me for. A thing I'm not sure I ever enjoyed." Clifford pulled at his neck.

"My father hated motorcycles. Said only bad boys and gang member rode them. Such nonsense. Took me eighty-one years to realize I am more than my folks' expectations. But I guess better late than never. So I will be getting back on the bike."

"Not for a few weeks at least." Miranda pointed to the broken wrist. "And the ulcer?"

"Doc's got me on meds. It's bleeding less. I might have to do surgery but to be honest I don't want to."

"It's laparoscopic now. Three little holes."

"Yeah. Yeah." Clifford waved her notes away. Clearly, that was something his gastroenterologist had explained, too. "Took me eighty years to live. Don't want to miss a moment."

"That sounds like a good plan." Miranda took a big breath. "A very good plan."

She and Knox were talking tonight. She wanted

to know exactly why he wanted this. If it was just to prove he was good enough, well, she wasn't sure how to make him realize he was already pretty perfect. But that was an issue to cross later.

Rumor is that someone named Ryann Oliver is putting in.

Ryann Oliver. Knox frowned as he read the name again. His friend in human resources wasn't in charge of hiring but he'd let Knox know when he heard rumors.

Ryann Oliver? That wasn't a surgeon he knew. Wasn't a surgeon he'd even heard of. What was their specialty? What did their CV look like?

His eyes floated to Miranda's front door. She'd asked for tonight to just be about them. He wanted to honor that, even though the competition was making his blood pump. He hadn't realized she needed a break.

The old Miranda wouldn't have.

Knox pinched the bridge of his nose, forcing the thought from his mind. It wasn't even accurate. The Miranda he'd competed against as a resident would have needed the break; she just wouldn't have asked for it.

And this wasn't even her competition.

One quick Google search and Ryann's name popped right up. Great. He'd get the basics about Dr. Oliver and then start his actual search tomorrow. Anything to get a leg up.

Ortho. What was it with the bone docs putting in for the position?

Knox read over Ryann's CV and his stomach sank a bit with each line. The woman was impressive. In fact, he'd argue that she was easily the top candidate.

His phone dinged again, an email notification coming across the screen. HR at Beacon Mountain in Maine was asking when he could come out to interview.

Would having a counteroffer make a difference at Hope? Maybe...

A knock echoed on the window. Knox jumped and his cheeks heated as he met Miranda's gaze.

He watched her dark eyes scan his phone and saw the slight shake of her head.

Opening the door, he slid out, ready to make his case. "Listen, I wasn't looking at other women. Or I was but just one in particular."

Nope, that sounded worse than anything he could possibly have come up with.

Miranda put her hand over his mouth and shook her head. "I am not worried that you are looking at other women." Her eyes rolled and she pulled her hand back. "I am disconcerted that you are reading a CV in front of my place on the night I specifically asked for no job talk."

Miranda pulled the phone from his hand, biting her lip. "Let me guess. Ryann Oliver is your latest competition?"

They'd talk about this for ten minutes then he was all hers tonight. No more job talk. That would be a nice compromise. He leaned against the hood. "According to the rumor mill."

"The rumor mill?" Miranda raised an eyebrow. "Please. I know you mean Pedro Garcia in accounting."

"Yes." But Pedro wasn't who he wanted to discuss. "This is where all my focus should go."

"Why do you want this job?"

She'd asked that question this afternoon, too. And he'd answered. Why were they back to this?

"You know why I want this job."

"No." Miranda shook her head. "I know that you were hurt not be considered and have thrown yourself headfirst into this." She gestured to his phone then to the tablet that was poking out of his backpack. "Why do you want this job?"

Knox paused, sucking oxygen in. He must have needed a breath for longer than he realized. His brain blanked. "What do you mean?"

"It's not a hard question, Knox. Or it shouldn't be. You haven't left Hope."

I might. Others wanted him. Wanted him bad, but he wasn't yet willing to voice that.

He wasn't even sure why he was so tense about bringing it up. He was the unusual one. People moved all the time.

Knox pointed to her door. "Why don't we go in, order some pizza and chat?"

Miranda looked like she wanted to argue but she started for the door.

"Fine. Pizza and we talk while we wait for it." Miranda walked into her condo, grabbed her phone and ordered. "There, that's done. Now spill. Why do you want this job?"

"Why do you keep asking me that?" Knox crossed his arms, mirroring her defensive stance.

"Why don't you give me an answer?"

"Because it's obvious. Of course I want the job. It's the head surgeon job." It was what surgeons aspired to. How many times had he heard that over the course of his career? That was the pinnacle location. One only a few got to.

"Why don't you want it?" Two could play the question game. Pulling his hand across his face, he looked at her. "You should want this."

"No." Miranda's eyes floated to the bookshelf where her self-help books resided. "No. I am allowed to be happy where I am."

Fine. That was true. She had a good point.

"What happens if you don't get this job that you want so bad you can list all these reasons?"

Frustration flared. Why did she keep pushing this? "If that happens then maybe I take the job in Maine." That would show the Hope board.

"Maine. Job. What?" Miranda's head tilted then shook as she placed a hand over her heart.

He hadn't meant for that to pop out but in for a penny, in for a pound. "The day I had a conversation with Hugh a headhunter reached out. It happens."

"It does." Miranda pursed her lips then motioned for him to continue.

"I was frustrated and pissed. I'll admit it. So I reached back. One thing led to another and I have an interview at Beacon Mountain." It was weird to say the words out loud. He hadn't even decided if he was taking the interview. He'd rage applied. But if he didn't want the job, he would have turned down the interview like he'd done so many times before.

The color drained from her face. "Maine. Like the state, Maine." It was clear she needed some time to process.

"Yes." Knox nodded, and keeping his voice upbeat, he added, "Instead of heat like here, it's lots of snow. At least that's what HR told me."

"HR told you about the snow. Wow. So you've had more than casual chats with them. A rage apply is one thing but…" She pushed her hand through her hair. "When were you planning on telling me?"

"Now."

"Really? This was really the plan."

All the words were stuck in his throat. He wasn't sure. The Beacon Mountain job was moving much faster than the Hope one. He'd never really considered a job anywhere else.

Not for long anyway. It just happened, and for once he hadn't stopped it.

He reached for her and she stepped back. "Miranda."

"Applying for a job without telling me. In a state thousands of miles away." She bit her lip, then closed her eyes for a second. "Okay. I hope you get what you want, Knox. I do. But my life is here. And I want a partnership."

"We have a partnership, sweetie."

She flinched and his heart broke. "Miranda." He wanted to stop time. Pretend for a few minutes that she wasn't ending things. "It's a job. People apply all the time. You came here."

"I did. My sisters are here. My life, the one I want, is here."

"If I want to be a head surgeon, I can't stay here." The words were out and with it the truth he hadn't let himself acknowledge. "I can look at a place closer."

"Closer than Maine," Miranda laughed but there was no humor in the sound. "A world of possibilities and the first one you applied to is forever away. And you didn't tell me. I've lived that life. The one where I find out the major decisions at the end. Where I am not consulted. I'm not doing that again."

"I deserve the job, Miranda. I compete. I better myself. I reach for more. If I stop trying, then am I still me?"

"You do deserve it. And I can't answer that last question, only you can." She laid a hand on his cheek then pulled back. "I want you to get everything you want, Knox. Everything you deserve. If you go to Maine, you'll have to send me pictures of the snow. I miss it sometimes."

The camera notification on her doorbell went off. The pizza was here. Pizza for the night they were supposed to have.

"You should take the veggie with you." She didn't catch the sob on the end of the statement.

"Right." A flood of words rushed through his brain. Pleas, cries, promises he wanted to believe he could keep. Instead, he opened the door, tipped the pizza delivery person and passed her the meat pizza.

Knox looked at the veggie pizza pie in his hands, then turned and walked out, his heart cracking into a million pieces as he stepped into the early night air.

CHAPTER SEVENTEEN

"YOU STILL NOT TALKING?" Jackson slapped Knox's back as he stepped into the condo with a cup of coffee for him.

Jackson passed Knox the coffee then shook his head at Knox's small couch. "I'd say you need a bigger one but this one fits the two of us just fine."

And that was all he needed.

His brother was nice enough not to point that out. But the truth still stung. It had fit him and Miranda, too. Though they'd spent most of their time at her place. With Icy.

Two days ago. Two days since he'd seen her. Forty-eight hours and an eternity.

"Want to play darts?"

Jackson's pity question made Knox sigh. And it meant he must look nearly as bad as he felt. "You don't want to play darts."

"Never do. But you do, so I thought I'd offer." Jackson took a sip of his coffee. "You like competition."

"Not exactly a secret, brother." Knox was glad he didn't have to worry his surly mood was going to impact Jackson. They'd been through hell together. "An intricate part of my personality that not everyone can accept apparently."

"Mmm-hmm." Jackson took another drink, his dark eyes holding Knox's.

"Something you want to say?"

Jackson shrugged. "Is there something you want to say? You're the one that's sat over here in silence for the last two days."

"I haven't been silent." Close. But not completely silent. The difference wasn't really important, but still.

"Mmm-hmm."

He hated that noise. It was one Jackson made when he had a lot of thoughts but planned to say none of them. "Ever thought of moving to Maine?"

"Umm, no." Jackson cleared his throat. "Not the direction I thought this conversation was going, I'll be honest. Why Maine?"

"Beacon Mountain Hospital is there. They offered me an interview and sent me virtual tickets for next week to fly in and see the facility." Knox gripped the coffee cup so hard he wondered if the lid might pop off. This was further than he'd gotten in any interview process. By his choice.

If Hope didn't want him, others did. So why did the idea of even stepping on the plane send chills down his back? Why had he nearly said no thanks a hundred times? The tickets were refundable; he could back out anytime he wanted.

Jackson still didn't say anything.

"Nothing to add? Nothing?"

Jackson tilted his head, his dark eyes showing

so much wisdom that Knox suddenly wished there was a way to retract his statement. "Wow. I can't believe you'd leave."

"I mean I'd miss Hope. And living next to you. And the summer heat. And this place—first place I've owned. And Sally's Donuts and the Mulligans and tot nights and you. And—"

"And Miranda," Jackson added.

"And Miranda." He'd miss her for the rest of his life. "I need this. I think."

"You think?"

"Miranda kept asking me why I wanted the position yesterday."

"It's a good question." Jackson sipped his coffee but didn't add anything further.

"I'd be good at it." Knox stated the obvious, not sure why nothing else would come to his brain.

"Miranda would be great at the position, too, but she doesn't want it." Knox took another sip of his coffee, trying to piece together any of the rapidly firing thoughts through his brain. "I've never left. This is my home."

Home.

He looked around the condo, at his brother, the little turtle bank he'd painted with Miranda, the pictures of him with staff and friends from Hope. This was his home. Not the condo but Hope Hospital and Phoenix.

And Miranda.

His ears buzzed and his heart wanted to bust

out of his chest. Why the hell hadn't this realization come forty-eight hours before?

"I love working at Hope."

"But you can't be the head surgeon working at Hope." Jackson tapped his fingers on the edge of the couch. "Not without experience elsewhere. You could take a job for a few years, then compete when whoever they hire moves on."

"I don't want—" He caught the words before they exited his mouth. He didn't want to move on. He loved his life. After a childhood proving himself, he'd earned the right to just be happy with himself. It was his ego that was bruised by Hugh's assessment that he wasn't a good candidate.

His ego that had driven him to apply for positions he didn't truly want.

Applying to hospitals without even talking to the woman he loved.

His heart bled as his brain pummeled him with memories of Miranda wishing him the best. Telling him she hoped he got everything he wanted. When everything he wanted was standing in front of him.

"I think a battering ram just pushed through my soul." Knox pulled up his phone, deleted the apps he'd downloaded to help with job prep. Then he went to the kitchen and grabbed his tablet. The battery was close to dead. He plugged it in and started deleting the CVs and info he'd gathered.

His neck flamed as he saw how much was there.

She'd been right to ask for a free night. Right to voice her concerns. Then he sent his apologies to Beacon Mountain. He was staying at Hope.

"Patrick O'Sullivan will do a fine job." Jackson grabbed his keys from the table by Knox's front door, already surmising that Knox needed to leave—now.

Knox chuckled. "He might if Ryann Oliver wasn't putting in. She's Patrick's true competition."

"Ryann?" Jackson turned, his brother's eyes brighter than he'd seen in forever. "Ryann with two ns?"

"Yeah. Dr. Ryann Oliver. She's from the Pacific Northwest. Orthopedics. Do you know her?"

"Probably not."

There was more to that story, but Knox didn't have time to peel the layers back on the looks passing over his brother's face.

"I need to see Miranda, but we're going to talk about whatever—" he pointed to Jackson's face "—is making that smile reappear."

"I don't know a Dr. Ryann Oliver." His brother pushed the phone into his back pocket.

"Maybe not. But you do know a Ryann. And I am guessing she is the reason you haven't dated since you got back from Hawaii—over a year ago!"

Jackson looked at his wrist, hitting an imaginary timepiece. "I thought you had someplace to be."

His brother was right, but sometime soon he was going to find out who Ryann was.

* * *

Her phone dinged. Another note from a colleague reaching out to make sure she knew the position had opened this morning. Hugh, Patrick, three nurses and the ER tech so far had sent her messages.

She wasn't making a mistake but the fact that she knew they weren't blowing up Knox's phone infuriated her. Miranda had been back at Hope less than six months.

Yes, she had worked at three other hospitals. Yes, following residency she'd taken a prestigious fellowship. Yes, she was good at her job.

But Knox was great at his job. He knew everyone in the area. Had good working relationships with nearly every doctor. He cared about the patients and staff. By rights he should be a top choice, the one glaring at his phone as another ding went off.

And instead of throwing his hands up and storming off, something Lance would have done in an instant, he'd buckled down. Trying to find a way to prove them wrong.

And he'd applied for the job in Maine.

But was he really serious about taking it?

Miranda looked at the wall of self-help books she had. The wall where she reached when her life wasn't turning out the way she thought it should. When she doubted herself. There was no book for this, though.

Knox hadn't told her about the interview. About the rage applying. He'd shared so much with her. Things she knew he hadn't told others. If the interview in Maine was *that* important, he'd have told her.

She suddenly knew that with crystal certainty.

He wanted recognition. Deserved it. And he was hurt—which was normal.

And rather than address the hurt, rather than comfort him, she'd asked if he really wanted Hugh's job and then panicked when he'd told her about Maine.

Instead of thinking through why Knox wouldn't tell her, she'd leaned back on her old life. On the hurt Lance caused. And she'd reacted to protect herself. Instead of comforting the man she loved.

Rebuilding her life was fine but not if she built its foundation on the past.

And if Knox needed to leave? If what he needed was someplace new?

She looked at Icy and then around her condo. Then they'd try somewhere new and she'd come back here as often as possible.

Miranda took a deep breath and walked into the kitchen to grab her keys. She wanted to talk to Knox. Now.

The front door dinged and she called, "Come in," over her shoulder. One of her sisters was probably dropping something off. They'd checked in three times in the two days since she and Knox had parted ways. Each coming up with a different random excuse for why they "just happened to be in the neighborhood."

That was something she loved about being back here. Something she'd miss if they left. But hey, there were viral videos of family reunions for a reason. That could be fun, too.

Her phone dinged and she threw her hand up in the air, unintentionally releasing the book in it. "Why won't people stop texting me about that stupid job? They should be texting Knox. Begging him to apply."

"That is nice to hear." Knox's voice was smooth as his arms wrapped around her waist. He laid his head on her shoulder and just held her. His arms tightened as she turned in them.

He was here.

"But you're right. I don't want it, either." His lips pressed against her forehead.

"Come on." She must be imagining things. Knox was here, gazing at her as though she was the sun in all its glory. "It's okay to want it, Knox. Okay to rage apply and be ticked that your phone isn't ringing off the hook."

"Yes. But I'm happy where I am. This is my home. I'm content, and I like that. I like the feeling of being sure in my place in this world. Of not needing anything else. I just didn't like the idea of people saying I wasn't qualified.

"I am so sorry that I didn't tell you about Maine,

sweetie. I didn't expect it to move so fast. I rage applied then just kept going. It was nice to be wanted."

"Of course it was." He was saying all the right words. Everything her heart needed to hear.

"And the righteous anger on my behalf, that feels better than anything else. I love you. This is home. And I'm happy, with you. And without that job we can watch more trash game shows together."

"I love you." Miranda kissed his cheek. "But I should have talked rather than wishing you well when I found out about Maine. It made no sense, and rather than dig into it, I just sent you on your way. I let the hurt from my past tarnish my future." Miranda squeezed him tight. "Forgive me?"

"Absolutely." Knox let out a sigh. "So, I guess now we get to watch Patrick work a ton of extra shifts for the next few months while the board looks across the nation for the hire."

"And we can work our regular already long shifts, then eat pizza and veg on the couch with a judgy cat monitoring us."

"Sounds pretty perfect to me." Knox dropped his head, his mouth capturing hers.

"Me, too."

* * * * *

*Look out for the next story in the
Hope Hospital Surgeons duet*

Her Secret Baby Confession

*And if you enjoyed this story, check out
these other great reads from Juliette Hyland*

A Puppy on the 34th Ward
Tempted by Her Royal Best Friend
Redeeming Her Hot-Shot Vet

All available now!